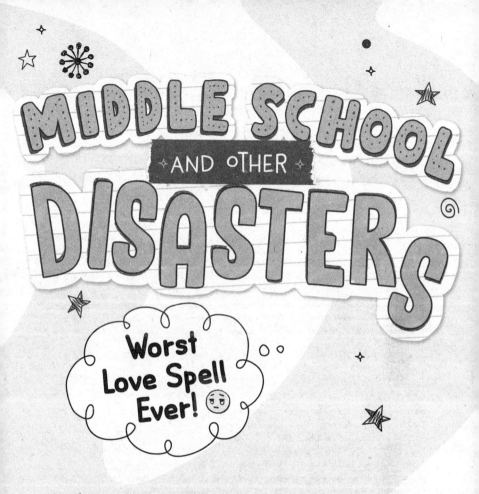

MIDDLE SCHOOL AND OTHER DISASTERS

Worst Love Spell Ever!

BY WANDA COVEN

ILLUSTRATED BY ANNA ABRAMSKAYA

Simon Spotlight

New York London Toronto Sydney New Delhi

SIMON SPOTLIGHT

An imprint of Simon & Schuster Children's Publishing Division

1230 Avenue of the Americas, New York, New York 10020

First Simon Spotlight edition August 2023

Copyright © 2023 by Simon & Schuster, Inc.

All rights reserved, including the right of reproduction in whole or in part in any form.

SIMON SPOTLIGHT and colophon are registered trademarks of Simon & Schuster, Inc.

For information about special discounts for bulk purchases, please contact Simon & Schuster Special Sales at 1-866-506-1949 or business@simonandschuster.com. The Simon & Schuster Speakers Bureau can bring authors to your live event. For more information or to book an event contact the Simon & Schuster Speakers Bureau at 1-866-248-3049 or visit our website at www.simonspeakers.com.

Text by Alison Inches

Series designed by Chani Yammer, based on the Heidi Heckelbeck series designed by Aviva Shur

Cover designed by Laura Roode

Illustrated by Anna Abramskaya, inspired by the original character designs of Priscilla Burris from the Heidi Heckelbeck chapter book series

The illustrations for this book were rendered with digital ink and a bunch of love.

The text of this book was set in Minou.

Manufactured in the United States of America 0723 FFG

10 9 8 7 6 5 4 3 2 1

Library of Congress Control Number 2023934736

ISBN 978-1-6659-3720-7

ISBN 978-1-6659-3721-4 (ebook)

To my readers:
You are magical.
Love,

Wanda

DREAM BOY

Little-known fact about me:

I absolutely love it when I wake up before my alarm.

It means one beautiful thing: *lounging in bed!*

Right now I have a whole half hour to luxuriate in my cool, crisp sheets while I listen to the birds sing, chirp, and call outside my window.

And best of all, I have time to think about the biggest, most important thing in the whole wide world right now—

my crush!

I've been thinking about him basically nonstop since my first day at Broomsfield Academy.

His name is Hunter McCann.

But I secretly call him Hunter McCutie.

I really like, like, *like* him!

I point my toes and swish my legs back and forth excitedly under the covers.

Eeeee! I squeal inside my head.

What if my crush turned into my boyfriend?

I am positively bursting with anticipation. Ever since I first saw Hunter, I've had a nonstop Fourth of July sparkler going off inside me.

Sizzle! Pop! Hiss!

It's like my whole being is filled with fizzing, popping heart-shaped candy!

Yup, I've got it BAD.

Okay, so how would I describe my dream boy, aka Hunter McCutie? Hmmm, let's see. Well, he's . . .

SuperCUTE!

Positively ADORABLE!

Chatty in a good way!

Deliciously drool worthy!

Totally hilarious!

Bewitchingly magical, as in he is a *wizard*!

Fun to be around.

Rocks a cool beachy style.

Strong and athletic.

And did I mention he's SO SUPERCUTE?!

Hunter is from California and has that effortless endless-summer surfer look, with honey-colored bangs, freckles, and a swagger that is always ON.

The best part of all is that I think he likes me too.

Or at least I hope so!

Because he's sweeter than sweet, and I know we'd make the perfect couple.

Wow, I can just imagine our picture in the yearbook. Hearts EVERYWHERE . . . !

Zeeeep!

Zeeeep!

Zeeeep!

Aack!

That horrifying sound is my alarm clock, and it just popped my beautiful daydream like a cat claw in a balloon.

I had to buy an alarm clock for boarding school because we're not allowed to have our phones during the week.

"Heidi, please turn that killer-bee buzzing sound OFF!"

That's my roommate, Melanie Maplethorpe, who is my former BEF (best enemy forever). She's also from my hometown of Brewster.

We got the shock of our lives when we moved into Broomsfield Academy only to discover that we were roommates—or rather broommates.

What were the chances of THAT happening?

If that isn't incredible enough, I also found out that Melanie is a witch, like me!

And there's MORE madness to this story!

Melanie and I learned that we actually have a lot in common, so now we're kinda, sorta *friends.*

We're not *best* friends, like Lucy Lancaster and me, but I think it's safe to say we're *friends in progress.*

Wham!

I hit the button on my alarm.

Then Melanie's alarm goes off.

Bling-a-ling-a-ling!

Bling-a-ling-a-ling!

Melanie has a retro pink alarm clock with two silver bells on top.

She whacks it with her hand, and the room goes quiet for a blissful second.

Then Melanie throws back her covers, rubs her
eyes, and slides into her pink fuzzy slippers.

Whisp! Whisp! Whisp!

I hear her slippers scuff into the bathroom. She's
always the first one up. I'm the lounger.

As I lie in bed, I think about what to wear.

Now that it's full-on fall, it's a little chilly, so I'm going to wear my new sweater. It has wide sage-green stripes, thin black stripes, and medium-wide cream stripes. I'll wear it with black leggings and a matching green headband. *Done!*

Then I roll over and—
oops!—fall back to
sleep.

Zzzzzzzzz.

I wake up in a panic.
Melanie is long gone,
but her flowery-fruity
perfume lingers. I look
at my clock.

*Oh no! I only have twenty minutes to
get ready and
go to class!
Eeek!*

I leap out of bed and
summon my outfit
with magic.

The outfit flies from
my drawers and onto
my bed.

I'm not supposed to use magic outside class unless it's for homework, **but I simply must use it right now or I'll be totally late!**

My clothes follow me into the bathroom. I splash my face with water, dress, and push my hair back with my headband. I give myself a quick magical manicure: French tips today. Then I fan my fingers and admire my work. **So cute!**

Okay, gotta go!

I grab my backpack and zip down the sidewalk to the Barn—that's where the cafeteria is. I don't have time for breakfast, but I do have a few seconds to spare to check the seating assignments. Each student is assigned new classmates to sit with every so often. It's a great way to get to know everyone in your grade. I always love to see who's at my table. Maybe Hunter will be at my table this week.

Fingers crossed.

When I get to the cafeteria, everybody's leaving for class. I run my finger down the table assignments. I'm at Table 1, which is Jenna's table. She's the resident advisor in my dorm, and she's totally awesome.

I go down the list some more.

Sunny and Annabelle are at my table!

Sunny and Annabelle are roommates. I met Sunny at the beach one summer, long before we came to Broomsfield Academy. I was so happy to see her on my first day here. She introduced me to Annabelle, and we all became fast friends. I'm so happy they'll be at my table.

And oh my gosh! Hunter McCutie is at my table too! *Swoon!*

Then my heart totally deflates because Melanie is also at my table. It's not that I don't like her. It just stinks because she has a HUGE crush on Hunter too.

MERGS to that!

I've had to keep my crush a secret from her, since we're crushing on the *same* guy.

The last thing I want is for Melanie and me to slip back into despising each other again.

But how can I talk to Hunter with Melanie at the table?

Rats-a-roni!

Melanie brushes by me on her way out of the cafeteria. She's talking to a girl named Isabelle Summer. Isabelle is captain of the girls' soccer team here at Broomsfield Academy. She has beautiful dark, curly hair and wears it in a high ponytail.

She's effortlessly pretty.

Melanie and Isabelle smile as they walk by. I smile back and dash to the cafeteria counter to grab a granola bar. I definitely don't need my stomach growling in class.

One word: *mortifying!*

As I race to class, I remember I have to pick a famous person to write about for social studies.

It's called a luminaries report. A luminary is an inspiring person of brilliant achievement. There are so many famous people from history who inspire me. I'm having a lot of trouble deciding.

I'm pretty much lost in my thoughts when THIS happens. . . .

CLONK! I bonk into somebody.

Aaagh!

Then I look up.

I've crashed right into Hunter!

Double aaagh!

Now I have a beet-red face to go with my red hair.

I wonder if there's a way to use magic to rewind this horrifying encounter!!!

But before I can figure that one out, I see Hunter's sparkling green eyes. His face crinkles with laughter. He's not mad at me or even annoyed. He thinks our sudden encounter is FUNNY!

"Wow, Heidi!" he says. "What planet are you on this morning? Are you okay?"

I laugh like a goofy cartoon character.

One word: *awkward.*

"Sorry, Hunter!" I manage to say. "I'm fine. I was thinking about my social studies assignment. Are you okay?"

He nods, and he's *still* laughing. Maybe he thinks I'm funny!

Or maybe he's laughing AT me.

We both jump when the bell rings. I shift my backpack up on my shoulder. "We'd better run, or we'll be late for class!" I say.

Hunter and I take off.

He's wearing khaki shorts and a pink polo frayed at the hem. He totally puts the chic into his shabby-chic beach look. **I love it!**

"We can make it if we hurry!" he says.

I'm chasing Hunter McCutie across campus! It's weird and wonderful.

English hasn't started as we slide into our seats. *Phew!*

Note to self: write to Lucy and tell her I crashed into my crush.

It's SO hard to sit still in class. I feel like a Christmas tree that just got plugged in. Every part of me is blinking and swirling, and I'm trimmed with excitement. I tell myself to chill about a hundred times, but that's like telling a popcorn machine to stop popping.

Heidi, you're a calm, all-together middle schooler.

I WISH.

And why do I keep hearing Hunter's name over and over?

Hunter McCann. Hunter McCann. Hunter McCann.

Am I losing my mind?

Nope. I'm not losing it, **because it's not *my* voice!**

I look around the room. That's weird. Nobody is talking, but I still hear the voice, and what's more, I *know* that voice.

Then it hits me.

It's *Melanie's* voice!

I'm not used to hearing other people's thoughts yet.

Reading minds is my gift as a witch.

The only problem is that I just discovered my gift and I have no idea how it works. For example, I never know when I'll tune in to someone else's thoughts. It just happens.

And it's happening right now!

And guess what Melanie is thinking about?

Hunter.

Merg!!!

Why do we have to like the same person?!

I zoom in on her thoughts. Now that I know it's
Melanie, her thoughts are coming in loud and clear.

She's staring at Hunter from across the room and thinking: *One day we'll get married!*

Seriously? I think.

Melanie is thinking about marriage in middle school?

Okay, that's way over the top. I keep listening. . . .

And when we have children, they'll be so gorgeous. They'll probably be supermodels. Everyone will stop and stare!

I cough to get Melanie off her train of thought.

It's too much.

I feel a little sick to my stomach.

I can't wait to learn in my magic classes how to control my gift of being able to read minds.

For now my coughing does the trick, and Melanie starts paying attention to the teacher.

My thoughts, on the other hand, start drifting away.

I wonder if Hunter and I like the same things.

Does he like mint-chocolate-chip ice cream like me?

Or the color blue?

Is his favorite animal a dolphin?

"Hei-i-i-di-e-e?" I hear a voice call my name from far, far away. "Heidi Heckelbeck? Would you care to join us?"

I come back to earth and look at my teacher
Ms. Langley. She laughs.

"Heidi, please turn to chapter six." I flip through
my book to find the right page. The pages slap
loudly as everyone waits for me to catch up.

Someone snickers.

Ever since I started having a crush, **my head
has been in outer space.**

Since when did my favorite subject become *boys*?

Okay, make that **one** *certain* **boy.**

But the more pressing question is: How am I going to make this **one certain boy** like me? And what if he likes Melanie better?

I have so many things on my mind.

No wonder it feels like I'm floating in outer space!

FLiRTiNG LESSONS

As I rush into the cafeteria for dinner, I see Annabelle and Sunny waving at me. They know I tend to run late, so they saved me a seat next to them.

I glance at the table and see Melanie sitting across from Hunter, batting her eyelashes at him.

UGH.

I'm going to skip flirting/crushing for this meal and just enjoy time with my friends.

Sunny doesn't seem to be living up to her name right now.

She's not smiling. Instead she's looking sadly down at her plate.

"Oh no! The food can't be that bad," I joke. I glance down at my tray, and it actually looks pretty good to me.

Tonight's dinner is lemon chicken, with mashed potatoes and steamed broccoli on the side.

"No, it's not that," Sunny says, and she even takes a bite of her chicken to show me.

"Then what's wrong, Sunny?" Annabelle asks, and she puts a hand gently on Sunny's arm. "Whatever it is, you can tell us."

Sunny lets out a huge sigh. "It's just a lot harder than I thought it would be."

"What is?" I ask.

"Witchcraft!" Sunny says.

"I was so looking forward to coming to Broomsfield because I was sure I was going to be the greatest witch they ever had," Sunny continues. "But I'm struggling in all my magic classes. My spells only work for a little while or not at all, and I can't memorize the potions I need. I nearly flunked the first potions test!"

Sunny keeps her head down, but she wipes the corners of her eyes.

Oh no! Sunny is crying!

"Maybe Broomsfield isn't for me," she whispers.

"Sunny, no!" I say. I feel so bad that she thinks she doesn't belong here.

"Listen," I continue. "It's been hard for all of us to adjust. We're living here and also studying our magic skills for, like, the first time ever."

Annabelle nods. "Plus," she whispers, "it's hard keeping such a big secret from all the non-magical kids at the school."

I didn't think of that, but Annabelle is totally right. Broomsfield Academy is the only school in the country for magical students, but there are also a lot of non-magical students who go here.

The School of Magic teachers have cast many spells so that the other students don't find out about the magic going on all around them, and the magical students have been sworn to secrecy. That's why we can't practice magic outside class.

It's fun sharing a big secret with my classmates, but it can also be a little stressful.

"Sunny, we will help you practice your magic," Annabelle continues. "Don't you dare even think of leaving!"

She gives Sunny a big hug, and I reach around Annabelle to squeeze Sunny's hand.

"We are all in this together," I say.

Sunny looks up and gives us a small smile.

"Thank you," she says. "You two always know how to make me feel better."

"There's nothing we can't do if we help each other," Annabelle tells Sunny.

"Speaking of help," I say, "can you both help me with *this*?" And I nod my head in Melanie's direction while she hangs on Hunter's every word.

Annabelle looks over and then turns back to me and Sunny. "**The only thing you should be around Hunter is yourself,**" she tells me. "If he likes you, then great. And if not, **there will be someone even better who does.**"

Sunny smiles. "I agree.

"Here's to Heidi.

"And Annabelle.

"And me!"

It's so good to see Sunny happy again!

And with that, I give Sunny a huge smile and decide I'm going to have a great dinner with my friends and not worry about my crush!

✧ ✧ ✧

I race to my desk after dinner and whip out my stationery from Aunt Trudy. I study each card and pick one with a pistachio-green border and my name in pink letters at the top.

So cute!

I grab a pink felt-tip pen.

Time to SPILL.

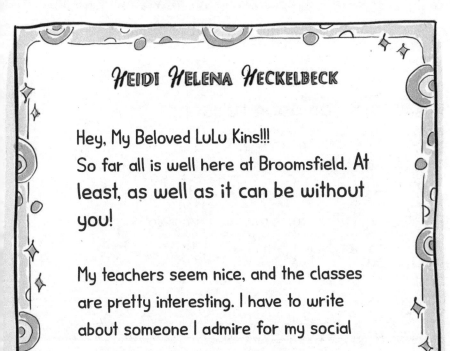

HEIDI HELENA HECKELBECK

Hey, My Beloved LuLu Kins!!!
So far all is well here at Broomsfield. At least, as well as it can be without you!

My teachers seem nice, and the classes are pretty interesting. I have to write about someone I admire for my social studies class. I wish I could write about YOU!

How are things going with you? As usual I am all over the place and upside down and inside out!

And you'll NEVER believe what happened to me on the way to class this morning.

It was a CLASSIC Heidi move, and it was all because I was a little inside my head.

But for good reason!

I was thinking about my social studies assignment. I was also on the verge of being late for class, so I was walking faster than normal. And that's when it happened. . . .

HEIDI HELENA HECKELBECK

I totally crashed into my crush, Hunter McCutie!

I mean, KA-BLAM!

How did I not see him?!

I was SO embarrassed.

Hunter must think I'm a total mess!

But he didn't get mad and say, "Watch where you're going!" He LAUGHED. He actually thought it was hysterical. He asked if I was okay too. And aside from feeling idiotic, I told him I was fine.

He was fine too. SO FINE!

Then BRRRRRING!

The bell rang, and we had to run to class.
I was actually chasing my crush!

Lol!

And I think we had a connection!
But who knows?

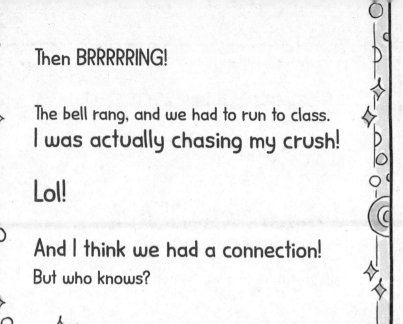

HEIDI HELENA HECKELBECK

Maybe the only connection we had
was slamming into each other, but I had
major sparks go off inside me, which is
nothing new, **because I've been
feeling sparks for him ever
since we first met.**

**But there's a HUGE
problem.**

Her name is Melanie Maplethorpe.

Surprise! Surprise!

She likes Hunter too, and has since the first week of school, like me.

MERG.

Melanie is so pretty. I'm sure Hunter is dazzled by her looks alone.

𝓗EIDI 𝓗ELENA 𝓗ECKELBECK

So all this adds up to my one burning question:

How can I get Hunter McCutie to like ME?

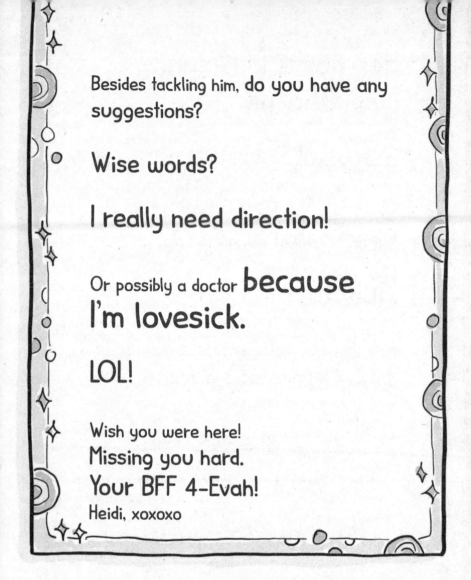

Besides tackling him, do you have any suggestions?

Wise words?

I really need direction!

Or possibly a doctor because I'm lovesick.

LOL!

Wish you were here!
Missing you hard.
Your BFF 4-Evah!
Heidi, xoxoxo

I tuck the letter into an envelope and peel and seal the flap.

Time to decorate!

I press a double-heart sticker that says "LOVE" onto the back of the envelope, and I put another sticker that says "Good Vibes" in puffy letters on the front.

I also put a stamp on it—even though I have no intention of walking all the way to the mail room to send it.

Regular mail will take *forever*, and I need answers ASAP.

I know we aren't supposed to use magic outside our classrooms, but Lucy needs to read this letter immediately!

I perform some quick mail magic, and my letter sails out the window.

Done!

And just in time!

The doorknob to our room twists. That means Melanie is back!

I quickly pull out my English assignment. She walks in and drops her pink-and-white book bag onto the floor beside her desk.

"What's up, Heidi?" she asks.

I shake my head. "Oh, nothing much—just thinking about what emotion to do my sense poem on."

Our English assignment is kind of tricky. You have to write about an emotion using each of your five senses: sight, sound, taste, smell, and touch. So for happy, you'd have to write about what happy looks like, sounds like, tastes like, etc.

It's fun, but challenging.

"How about doing yours on love?" Melanie suggests.

Then Melanie pauses and gives me a look. "When are you going to tell me WHO your mystery crush is?"

I shake my head. "That's still top secret information!"

I'm not about to tell Melanie I like the same guy SHE likes.

Eeek!

Melanie shrugs.

"No biggie," she says—even though she's dying to know. "The real question is: Are you making progress?"

I sigh heavily.

"Zero progress," I admit. "I don't know the first thing about getting him to like me. I am a total beginner at love."

Melanie laughs. "Well, you know you have to flirt with him, *right*? That's the only way you'll find out if he likes you back."

I frown.

"I don't know anything about flirting, and besides, I'm sure I would mega embarrass myself."

Which, of course, I've already done.

A sly smile forms on Melanie's face, and she runs over and plunks onto my bed.

"You're in luck!" she says. "Because it just so happens, I'm an EXPERT at flirting. It's an ancient art form, you know. The trick is to be subtle."

I slap my forehead with my palm.

Of course Melanie is an expert on flirting!

And I'm sure she'll attract Hunter McCutie into her charming web of love.

Then it dawns on me—if Melanie teaches me some of her flirting techniques, maybe I can beat her at her own game!

"Do you think you could share some flirting tips with me?" I ask innocently.

Melanie's face lights up, and she pounces on my invitation.

"Of course I can!" she cries.

Then she launches right into to Flirting Lesson Number 1.

"The first thing you have to do is flash your gorgeous smile. Come on. Let's see it, Heidi. Show me your *best* smile."

I sit next to Melanie and try to give her my most bewitching smile, but my face muscles won't cooperate. I just know that I end up looking like I feel—shy, nervous, and confused.

We both crack up.

"AGAIN!" Melanie commands.

I force another smile, and **this one is cheesier than in my last yearbook photo.**

Melanie laughs so hard that she snorts, which, of course, makes *me* snort too.

Then Melanie goes right back into teacher mode.

"Okay, so the next thing you have to do is sprinkle your crush with compliments. Find stuff you like about him and then say something nice," Melanie explains.

"Now pretend I'm your crush and give me a compliment."

I look at Melanie, and it's so hard not to laugh.

"Hey-y-y-y, Melanie." My voice cracks because I can barely hold it together. "That's a really nice top you're wearing."

Melanie giggles and nods approvingly.

"That's it!" she says. "And by the way, thanks for
the compliment—*wink, wink.*"

We break into more giggles.

Then she hops off the bed and walks to the other side of our room.

"This next move is something I do *all the time*," she says. "Before I enter a room where my crush is, I do a hair flip first, like this. I read in a fashion magazine that this is what some models do before they have their photo taken."

Melanie bends over so her hair hangs down, like a mop. Then she whips it back up.

She does this three times in a row.

Her hair looks wild and glamorous.

"I call this the 'windblown effect.' Your turn, Heidi!"

I have to admit, Melanie's "windblown effect" looks really good on her, so I stand up and flop my hair upside down. Then I whip it back up. I do this three times, like Melanie did. Then I cup my hand under my hair and do a goofy pose.

Melanie laughs.

"That's it!"

I sit back down. "Is there *more*?"

Melanie nods. "Of course there's more! Another thing boys love are BIG eyes."

Melanie widens her eyes. She looks beautiful, of course.

Could she ever look less than beautiful?

I mimic Melanie and hold my eyes wide open.

Instead of a glamourous girl, I probably look like an owl.

"That's pretty good!" Melanie praises.

I have to say, **it's so much more fun to be Melanie's friend than her enemy.**

Melanie continues, "And you should always have good posture, too. It makes you look confident." Melanie stands up straight and struts across the room like a runway model.

When I try it, I feel like a **clumsy baby giraffe learning to walk.** Melanie shakes her head at me like, *You're hopeless, Heidi.*

"Okay, another great flirting tip is the head toss. You giggle and throw your head back, but just a little."

Melanie demonstrates the head toss, followed by some gentle fake laughter.

I'm not sure I can pull this one off either, but come to think of it, when somebody tells a bad joke, I can do a pretty good fake laugh.

So I toss my head back and laugh, but it sounds totally foolish. *"Ha, ha, ha, ha!"*

It's so bad that Melanie rolls her eyes and we burst out laughing again.

So far my flirting skills are **one word:** *pathetic.*

Next Melanie runs across the room and grabs her desk chair. She wheels it over next to me.

"Heyyyy," she says like she's interested in me. Then she points her feet in my direction.

"Did you see that little move?" she asks. "Always point your feet in the direction of your crush. It says, 'You're someone I'd like to get to know better.'"

I turn my feet toward Melanie. I also point both index fingers at her at the same time and giggle. I can't help it. Melanie frowns.

"No, Heidi! That's TOO obvious!"

Melanie gives me another command. "This last one is very important. **You have to ask your crush questions so you can learn more about him.** It's fun to find out if you have stuff in common. You can also make little jokes about classes, homework assignments, school food—*you know.*"

I nod. Melanie sure knows her stuff. "Where did you learn all this?"

Melanie laughs. "I didn't learn it! I was born with it!"

I believe it.

"Have you ever thought about writing a *real* guide to flirting?" I ask. "I bet it would be a bestseller!"

Melanie lights up. "That's a great idea, Heidi! I have so much material. That would be amazing.

"It would probably win awards. As for you, **just remember: practice makes perfect!**"

I know Melanie is right. I'm going to have to employ these flirting techniques first thing tomorrow.

Whatever it takes to win Hunter's affection.

And P.S. May the best girl win!

It's a good thing Melanie doesn't know she's competing with me.

Lol!

Eek!

Girl power?

Melanie unpacks her book bag and sets up her homework on her desk. Her computer starts beeping.

She turns around and gives me an intense look. I raise my eyebrows. "What?"

Melanie turns off the alarm on her computer. "We have that meeting in Jenna's room *right now*! We'd better get going!"

Whoa, I had totally forgotten about the meeting.

We hurry down the hall to Jenna's room and knock on her door.

"Come on in!" Jenna calls. We open the door and find our RA doing a saddle stretch, with both legs out to the sides, and her head bowed to the floor. Her chestnut-brown beach curls are displayed on the floor in front of her.

She pops up and gives us her cheerleader smile.

"Hey, you two! Have a seat!"

Jenna has a room to herself, complete with her own personal living room.

We plop onto the couch. There's a plate of brownies on the coffee table and a pitcher of ice water with cucumber slices floating in it.

Fancy!

"Help yourselves!" Jenna says as she sits down on a chair with oversize cushions.

Melanie pours cucumber water into the glasses. Then we all help ourselves to brownies.

"I have some really fun news for everyone!" Jenna begins. "Broomsfield is going to hold the first dance of the year this weekend!"

Melanie and I look at each other with wide eyes.

"And it's a Halloween dance, so everyone gets to dress up in costumes," Jenna adds.

Melanie and I both squeal.

A costume dance! I love to dress up! But I've never been to a dance before.

I wonder if Hunter will dance with me! Then I realize that Melanie is probably wondering the same thing.

Oh, merg!

Jenna grabs a folder and pulls out flyers with all the details of the Halloween dance.

The flyers have images of ghosts, witches, and mummies dancing in the background.

All I can think is, *How will I be able to dance with Hunter if Melanie is there? Or worse, what if* she's *dancing with him the whole time?*

Hmmm. Maybe Melanie will have an emergency that night and won't be able to go.

Then I catch myself.

No magic, Heidi!

Jenna holds one of the flyers up. "We need to get the word out about the dance right away. I'm asking all my residents to pitch in with various assignments. Would you two help hang flyers around school for me?"

Melanie and I both nod like crazy.

How fun that *we* get to be the ones to spread the news about the first dance of the year!

"YES!" we say at the same time.

Then Jenna splits the flyers into two equal stacks and hands one stack to me and the other one to Melanie. "Great! I *knew* I could count on you two!"

Then Jenna tells us about past dances as we eat our brownies and drink our fancy water.

Later, on the way back to our room, Melanie goes on and on about her costume.

"I already know what my costume will be!" she says excitedly. "I'm going to wear a super cool mod dress like they wore in the 1960s!

"A multicolor daisy-print dress, shiny white boots, and lots of jangly jewelry! It'll be shimmery and super-groovy! I also have a clip-on ponytail to make my hair really BIG.

"Hunter will FLIP when he sees me!

"Don't you think we're a TRUE match, Heidi?!"

She barely pauses before she adds: "So, what are you going to be?!"

I sigh heavily.

I think some love just leaked from my heart.

Should I go ahead and give up on Hunter right now?

Melanie is definitely going to win. I don't stand a chance.

Maybe I should go to the dance dressed as wallpaper, because that's how noticed I'll be.

"I'm not sure what costume I'll wear," I say. Then I turn and look out the window. It's fall, and the leaves are beginning to turn.

Well, I'm turning too—only, the color I'm turning is green with jealousy.

Hey, maybe THAT'S the emotion I should write my sense poem on!

3

MISSION OF LOVE

"I'm taking control of my crush!"

Those are the first words out of Melanie's mouth the next morning. She pulls off her eye mask— *her latest nighttime accessory*—and drops it onto the nightstand. "And *you* should take control of *your* mystery crush too! Remember, we're in this together!"

I laugh to myself. *Together?! We're more "in this together" than she'll ever know!*

Wow, crushing on the same guy is hard enough, but keeping it a secret from Melanie is even harder! I have to constantly remind myself to be careful.

Melanie suddenly sits up in bed. "I have an *amazing* idea, Heidi. Will you help me?"

I roll over and look at Melanie. "*Maybe*. What's your idea?"

Melanie hops out of bed and grabs her stack of dance flyers. "I want to use these flyers as an excuse to spy on Hunter. We can hang them up in his dorm and maybe learn more about him. Will you come with me so it won't look like I'm spying?"

I jump out of bed and rush to the bathroom and start brushing my teeth so I can think privately.

Okay, why would I help Melanie find out stuff about MY crush?

Answer: because then I would be learning stuff about him too!

One word: *brilliant.*

I shout from the bathroom, "I'd love to help!"

Melanie claps her hands. "Oh, thank you, Heidi! We can call it **Melanie's Mission of Love!**"

No! I shout inside my head. *We can call it Heidi's Mission of Love because Hunter McCutie and I are soon to become the Dynamic Love Duo.*

But, of course, I give Melanie the answer she wants to hear. **"That's a great idea, Melanie!"**

Melanie prances across the room to her closet. "Now to pick the perfect outfit!"

I rush out of the bathroom and race to my dresser because *I need the perfect outfit too!*

Melanie and I get dressed and stand side by side in front of the mirror. Our outfits are *very* different. I have on a frayed jean skirt with embroidered flowers, a periwinkle-blue top, a white jean jacket, and plain white sneakers.

I think it's so cute until I compare it to Melanie's outfit.

She has on a white cotton jumpsuit with adorable little shoulder straps. There are hand-painted flowers and greenery on her pant legs and the sweetest little butterfly just above the flowers. There's another butterfly just below one shoulder strap. She wears a light pink T-shirt underneath, with a matching pink cardigan and sandals.

How does Melanie do it? She always looks stylish and perfectly put together.

One word: *envious.*

We both push our hair back with headbands—my headband is periwinkle to match my shirt, and hers is pink, of course. Melanie rubs creamy pink blush onto my cheeks and smears strawberry lip gloss across my lips, which I named "unicorn snot" the first time Melanie ever put it on me, but the shine is nice.

Then she does her own face and spritzes herself with perfume. Melanie's gift as a witch is potions, so she has tons of fragrances. She squirts a zesty citrus spray onto my wrist. Then we freshen our fingernail polish with magic, grab our dance flyers and some tape, and head to the Barn for breakfast.

Even though we're after the same guy, I feel pretty good today. I also have butterflies in my stomach because I'll see Hunter at breakfast.

I'm so happy he's at my table this week!

Eeee!

As Melanie opens the door to the Barn, she stops and looks over her shoulder at me. "Remember, watch and learn from my flirting techniques."

We step into the hallway, and no one's around, so Melanie stops again. "Let's do some hair flips before we go in."

We both take off our headbands, bend over, and whip our heads back and forth.

Flip! Whip! Flip!

The windblown effect is now fully engaged.

We slip our headbands into our backpacks and enter the cafeteria.

I spy Hunter right away. He's sitting in between Isabelle and Tate Harris, a good friend of Hunter's from his baseball team.

Melanie runway-walks to our table and sits across from Hunter, just like she did yesterday. I watch her closely.

She's already in full flirting mode.

I sit with Sunny and Annabelle, which isn't a bad thing. I love my Broomsfield friends. It's just that I wanted to sit next to Hunter this morning.

I keep watching Melanie out of the corner of
my eye. She's already used all her flirting
techniques in less than five minutes.

She's flashed her smile,

batted her big eyes,

tilted her head and giggled,

and complimented Hunter.

Melanie is a true pro.

I turn to Sunny and Annabelle.

"Be right back." I dash to the cereal bar and pour a bowl of crunchy oats and milk. It sloshes as I walk back to the table.

I'd better not spill, or Hunter will *really* think I'm a klutz.

I set my bowl on the table and sit down. Sunny and Annabelle are already finished eating, so all eyes are on me.

Sunny seems back to her usual sunny self. "Sunny, what's up?" I say. "You're positively glowing!"

Sunny turns to look at Annabelle. "Annabelle helped me study my potions last night," she says. "I think I'm going to ace my next test."

Annabelle beams at Sunny. "You're going to do great," she says. "I can feel it!"

"That's terrific, Sunny," I say. I pause and take a quick look around the table to make sure no one else is listening to our conversation.

"So you'll never guess what happened yesterday on the way to class," I whisper, dipping my spoon into my cereal and shoveling a spoonful into my mouth.

Sunny and Annabelle look at each other and smile.

"Spill!" Sunny says.

I finish munching and lean in closer.

"I accidentally crashed into Hunter on the way to English," I whisper. "I wanted to tell you last night at dinner, but I was afraid Melanie would hear. But now I can see she's not paying attention to us at all."

Sunny slaps the table and laughs. I put my finger to my lips.

"Shhhh!" I say. "Don't call attention to me!"

But Sunny doesn't get it. "Well, that's *one* way to get to know him!" she says in almost a normal voice.

I kick Sunny under the table.

"Shush! This is totally top secret!

"If *you know who* finds out my crush is *you know him*, we'll be enemies all over again."

Sunny looks toward the other side of the table at Hunter.

Not TOO obvious!

Then I hear Sunny speak to me with her thoughts. *It kind of looks like Hunter likes Melanie or Isabelle,* she thinks.

I wonder why I can hear Sunny's thoughts better than anyone else's. It's probably because I've known her longer than anyone else at Broomsfield, except for Melanie, and Melanie and I weren't friends until a few weeks ago.

I slurp a bite of cereal and nod. This time I look at the other side of the table.

I can't help it! Hunter is like a magnet.

And things are happening.

Isabelle just nudged Hunter.

Now she's whispering something to him.

Hunter shuts his eyes and bursts out laughing. Isabelle is laughing too.

What's so funny? I wonder.

Then I glance at Melanie, who's staring at her French toast. **She looks mad.** Wow, Sunny is right. Isabelle is also vying for Hunter's attention.

This is getting complicated.

Annabelle taps me on the arm. I jump and accidentally flick some cereal and milk onto the table. My friends laugh.

"Your head is in the clouds, Heidi!" Annabelle says in her charming British accent. She leans forward on her elbows.

"So what do you know about this boy?" Annabelle asks.

I shrug. "Not much," I whisper. "Just that he's cute, he's a wizard, and he picked a black feather at the Feather-Picking Ceremony at the start of the school year. Oh! He's from California and likes baseball and reading."

My friends just stare at me.

"That's IT?" Annabelle says. "Even I knew *that* much!"

I shrug and sneak another peek at the other side of the table.

Okay, so I need to find out more about Hunter.

I can see he likes French toast with strawberries. He also likes girls—or rather, girls like *him*. And of all the girls he knows, I appear to be the one in last place.

Merg.

This is depressing, so I switch topics. I tell Sunny and Annabelle about the dance this weekend and show them one of the flyers.

"This will be fun!" Sunny says.

Annabelle grabs the flyer. "I love a good masquerade party!"

Melanie walks over and taps me on the shoulder. "We have to get going," she says with a wink.

Sunny and Annabelle raise their eyebrows.

I grab my backpack and hang my tape around my wrist like a bracelet. "We're going to hang flyers for the school dance."

Sunny stands up and gathers her breakfast dishes. She sees my hands are full and grabs my cereal bowl, too.

"Thanks, Sunny!" I say.

As Melanie and I head out of the cafeteria, we bump into Hunter, but this time I don't body-slam him like I did yesterday.

"Hey, Hunter!" Melanie says in a singsong voice. "Wasn't that French toast amazing?"

Hunter smiles at both of us. "It wasn't bad for school food!" he says. "See you later!"

Hunter walks off to catch up with Isabelle.

Melanie clucks her tongue. "Isabelle is **definitely proving to be competition in my quest for Hunter.**"

I watch Hunter and Isabelle too. **This is turning into the Crush Olympics!**

And I'm going for GOLD!

Melanie grabs me by my arm. "Okay, Heidi—let's hang up some flyers and **get into spy mode!**"

We follow Hunter to see if he's going back to his dorm, but he and Isabelle head toward the lake. They're probably going to hang out and talk.

I am so jealous!

So is Melanie.

"I wish we could follow them," she says, "but I don't want to get caught spying on him, especially when he's with another girl." Melanie turns back to me. "So here's the plan. We'll save Hunter's dorm for *last.* Then hopefully we can meet up with him when he gets back."

Melanie is such a schemer, and her plan is *perfect.*

We go right to work and hang flyers EVERYWHERE. We hang them in all the dorms, the library, the Barn, the main office, the gym, and the auditorium. We even tape flyers on the walls in the hallways, on the classroom doors, and all over the School of Magic.

Now the only place left to go is Eaglesback, which is Hunter's dorm.

Here we go!

Melanie and I giggle as we approach. Spying is both terrifying *and* exhilarating.

I used to spy on my parents when I was little, and I was so scared of getting caught.

Now the stakes are higher.

Melanie and I quickly apply our lip gloss and flip our hair before we enter the dorm.

Eaglesback is an old building, like our dorm, Baileywick. The old buildings on campus are the coolest.

Melanie and I walk into the common area and check around for Hunter. He's not there, so we hang a flyer. Some of the kids ask us about the dance.

Then Melanie does something flat-out bold. She walks right up to some boys playing video games on a wide-screen TV.

"Excuse me!" she says confidently. "What room is Hunter McCann in?"

And you know what's amazing? One of the boys answers! "Room 201," he says, never taking his eyes off the screen.

And *blammo!* Just like that—we're IN!

Well not *in* Hunter's room, but at least we know where it is! We charge upstairs to the second floor and creep down the hall toward his room.

I wonder what will happen next!

We're now standing in front of Hunter's door.

I bite my thumbnail because it feels really awkward to be here. Melanie doesn't

care. She rests her ear against the door. Then she turns around and flaps her hands in the air wildly. "He's IN there! I heard noises!!!"

I yank her away from the door. "Melanie, what if he catches us out here?"

Melanie flips her hair again and walks back to his door. "All the better!"

I clench my fists. "Melanie, I swear, if you knock on his door, I'm going to make a run for it!

"I don't want to get caught!

"He'll think we're SO weird."

Melanie and I are arguing about our next move when Hunter's door opens.

We freeze, except for our mouths, which drop like drawbridges over a castle moat.

"Hi, Melanie! Hi, Heidi!" Hunter says, like seeing us standing outside his room is perfectly normal, which, of course, it's anything BUT. "What are you up to?"

Melanie regains her composure faster than I do. **She steps closer to Hunter.**

"Oh, hey, Hunter!" she says casually. "Heidi and I were hanging flyers for the Halloween dance this weekend! Have you heard about it?"

Hunter shakes his head. "Nope, but it sounds fun!"

Melanie hands him a flyer. He looks it over.

"Nice!" he says.

Meanwhile, I'm standing in the background, like the Statue of Dorkiness.

But I'm also a dork on a mission, and what comes out of my mouth next surprises even me. "Since we're here, Hunter, . . . can we see what a room in Eaglesback looks like?"

Hunter hesitates. He looks up and down the hallway. "I could get in trouble. We really aren't allowed to let any girls into our rooms. . . ." He looks around one more time to be sure it's safe. Then he grins. "Okay, one quick peek!"

Melanie pinches me as Hunter goes into his room.

"Nice move, Heidi!" she whispers.

I nudge her back. *Not a bad move at all,* I think proudly.

Melanie and I stand at the doorway and peek into Hunter's room. Hunter has a single room like Jenna does, but he's not an RA.

Lucky!

And his room has a baseball *and* California theme. He has baseball jerseys of his favorite players hanging on the walls, along with framed pictures signed by players, and a baseball cap collection. There's also a picture of palm trees at sunset, a framed flag of California, and a surfboard. A black-and-white canvas painting of a baseball bat and ball hangs over his bed.

But there's one thing in his room that completely melts my heart. There's a very worn and VERY cute little stuffed bear propped against his pillow. Melanie spies the bear too.

"I *LOVE* your teddy bear!" she cries before I
have a chance to say it myself.

Hunter laughs. "That's Bear-Z. I've had him since I
was a baby."

"Bear-Z is SO adorable!" But what she's *really*
saying is, *Hunter,* you're *so adorable!*

Hunter's cheeks turn
pink.

He rubs his hands together.

"Well, that's my room!" He
grabs one of his baseball
bats. "I'm off to the batting cage."

Melanie and I walk out of the building with Hunter.
He waves as he jogs toward the batting cage.

Melanie turns around and looks at me intensely.
"That was AMAZING, Heidi! And now I know Hunter
loves baseball, surfing, and all things California.

"Wow, I'm more into him than ever!"

I almost say, *Me too*, but catch myself.

"Well, Melanie's Mission of Love *accomplished*!" I say instead.

Melanie shoves me playfully. I shove her back.

We've made progress in love today, but has either of us taken control of our crush?

Two words: *Not yet.*

NO GUTS, NO GLORY!

Now it's time for ME to take action! I say to myself on the way to my spells and potions class later that day.

Because how will Hunter ever like me unless I show some SPUNK?

A spunky girl would ask her crush good questions.

And a super-spunky girl would simply ask her crush out.

But what if he rejects me? That would be a spunk-zapper, for sure.

But if I don't try *anything*, I'll be stuck in this bottomless crush swamp forever.

Three words: *Be bold, Heidi!*

I hold my library card in front of the fish's mouth on the fountain. This is one of the three secret entrances to the School of Magic, and my favorite one.

The door opens. A blast of cold air blows over me.

Aaaaah!

I sit at the top of the slide. My legs are sticky from the warm fall day, so my skin squeaks as I scootch myself forward on the metal slide.

But soon I pick up speed.

Wheeeeee!

I swerve around the curves until the slide flattens out at the bottom.

I hop off and head to spells and potions. As I enter the room, I zero in on Hunter. He's in the second row.

The sparkler inside me rekindles. *Hiss! Pop! Sizzle!*

Unfortunately, this wonderful feeling is followed by an instant buzzkill in the form of two immediate problems.

Melanie and Isabelle.

Melanie is sitting on Hunter's right, and Isabelle is sitting on his left. The needle on my crush-o-meter falls to zero.

I have to give myself a quick pep talk.

Come on, Heidi! You've got this! I tell myself. *If you have to compete for Hunter's love, then accept the challenge!*

Two words: *Challenge accepted!*

I take the seat *behind* Hunter—that way I can keep tabs on him *and* my competition. I pull out my notebook, and a pencil with a panda eraser on top. Then I catch Isabelle passing a NOTE to Hunter!

Are you kidding me?

Hunter clutches the note in his hand without taking his eyes off Mrs. Kettledrum, who hasn't started class yet. He unfolds the note and reads it.

I wish I knew what it said!

Hunter writes something back. Maybe it's just about homework. Isabelle reads his note. Then she smiles and covers her mouth. *It's clearly NOT about homework.*

They're totally flirting!

I kick the leg of my table. **Okay, that _does_ it!** Now I'm going to have to do something drastic to get Hunter's attention.

But what? Hmm, I'll have to let this simmer awhile.

So if Isabelle likes Hunter too, that means three girls are crushing on the same boy. At least three! Who knows how many other girls like him too. Merg!

Are Melanie and I **both** losing in our quest to win Hunter? Only time will tell.

Mrs. Kettledrum takes attendance. Her corgi, Momo, sits on her chair. Momo always comes to class, and everybody loves her. "Be a good girl, my little Momo Bear," Mrs. Kettledrum coos to her dog. Momo looks up at her adoringly.

Mrs. Kettledrum calls my name.

"Here!" I say in a bright cheery voice, because the last thing I want is for Hunter to think I'm boring, drab, and jealous. I may be an emotional yo-yo on the *inside*, but not on the outside!

After attendance Mrs. Kettledrum hands out spiral-bound booklets and—wait for it . . .

WANDS!!!

Ooohs and aaaahs go round the room.

Mrs. Kettledrum plops a booklet onto my table and hands me my very own shimmering wand. I grasp the wand in my hand, and it makes me feel powerful and grown-up, like **I'm an authentic, wand-carrying witch!** The handle has an amethyst in a six-prong setting on the end.

The meaning of an amethyst is to cleanse, protect, and inspire, according to Annabelle, who is an expert on crystals. After all, she has a treasure chest full of them, and she took the time to explain each crystal's meaning to me just last weekend.

Melanie's handle has pink quartz.

Hunter has black onyx.

And Isabelle's has a yellowish-green peridot.

Then I read the title on my booklet, *Elementary Spells and Potions*.

Seriously?!

"Elementary" means "for beginners."

I am *not* a beginner witch!

One word: *LAME*.

"Okay, class!" Mrs. Kettledrum says. "I want each of you to get acquainted with your new booklet and wand. Each wand has been hand-selected by our magical staff and is tailored specifically for you. Your homework assignment will be to choose a spell or potion from your booklet to be performed at our next class."

I thumb through my booklet. **These spells look SO easy**—much easier than the ones in my *Book of Spells*, which I've been using since I was little.

Merg. I want to be challenged as a witch.

Suddenly I hear a voice.

Hmmm . . . some of these spells are quite easy for my more advanced students.

I look around. **Who said that?**

I hear the voice again.

Well, I'll soon be assigning more difficult spells, but we have to start somewhere.

I realize I'm picking up Mrs. Kettledrum's thoughts. There goes my random mind-reading gift again! I love it, but it takes me by surprise every time.

I smile at Mrs. Kettledrum. I'm so glad she realizes that some students (like me!) need more of a challenge. But I still have to pick a spell or a potion from my booklet for homework.

I study the table of contents and see a chapter called "Potions of Attraction, Beauty, and Love." *Now* we're talking!

Maybe there's a spell in here that will help me get Hunter's attention!

Speaking of Hunter, he just raised his hand. Mrs. Kettledrum calls on him.

"Is there a spell that can help me hit a home run?" he asks.

Some kids laugh. Melanie slides her elbow on the table toward Hunter.

"That's SUCH a good idea, Hunter!" she says.

Hunter bobs his head and smiles. Melanie just used Flirting Tactic Number 2: complimenting your crush. And I have to agree—Hunter's question *is* a good one. How cool would it be if you could hit a home run every time you came to bat?

Mrs. Kettledrum chuckles like she's heard that question before.

"It might help you hit a home run once, Hunter, but these spells are short-term. Practice and muscle memory will help you hit home runs again and again."

Then Isabelle's hand shoots up. "Do spells work with penalty kicks, too?"

Mrs. Kettledrum nods. "But again, maybe once, Isabelle."

Now Melanie's hand is up and she waves it so violently, she practically falls off her chair. Mrs. Kettledrum nods toward Melanie.

"Is there a spell for making someone *super*-popular?" This time the whole class bursts into laughter.

Only Melanie would ask a question like *that*.

But secretly everyone wants to know the answer—even Momo barks. Mrs. Kettledrum pats her dog between the ears and continues.

"Yes, Melanie. There *are* spells of attraction. Spells as small as getting someone's attention or as big as getting a crowd to hang on to your every word, but you have to be careful. You may attract something that might not be right for *you.*"

Melanie looks unfazed. She's pretty confident when it comes to potions, and the only thing she wants to attract is Hunter.

Fingers crossed that she finds out Hunter is *not right* for her.

And toes crossed that I find out he *IS* right for me.

The girl sitting in front of Hunter, Sophie Rodriguez, asks if she can make her hair shorter with a spell. Mrs. Kettledrum tells Sophie it's more practical to get a *real* haircut, because this spell is temporary too. Then Hunter leans over his table and taps Sophie on the shoulder.

"I like your long hair, Sophie! Don't cut it!" he whispers, but it's loud enough so we can all hear it. Sophie turns around and smiles at Hunter. Her face turns pink.

And if my face could turn green, it would be green with jealousy, of course.

Why does every girl at Broomsfield Academy like Hunter McCann?!

Sheesh!

But then I realize something. Hunter's comment has revealed valuable *new* information! *He likes long hair!* Hmmm, I wonder. *If I had long hair, would Hunter notice ME?*

I open my booklet with renewed interest. Maybe there's a spell in here for long hair. . . .

The bell rings, so I'll have to continue my search later. I close my booklet. Suddenly the title changes to *Advanced Theoretical Equations in Astrophysics.* We all look up at Mrs. Kettledrum, and she smiles. "No, you all didn't just become scientists," she says. "I just like to ensure that non-magical students don't take an interest in our reading material!"

Ha! Mrs. Kettledrum thinks of everything.

Makes sense. As we file out of class, I accidentally brush against Hunter's arm.

Kaboom! My inner sparkler explodes into fireworks. And the best part? Hunter is looking right at me! Okay, I have his attention, so now to take action FOR REAL.

Four words: *Go for it, Heidi!*

"Hey, Hunter, you wanna get ice cream?"

Hunter's face lights up. "Always!"

I break into a smile, because it IS a great idea—that is, until Hunter asks Isabelle, Sophie, Melanie, and Tate to join us.

And they all say *YES*, of course.

Merg-a-roni!

Well, so much for taking action, but I definitely get an *A* for effort.

THE SECRET LOFT

After ice cream with Hunter **and the entire world,** I decide to go to the library for a while to work on my sense poem.

Annabelle and Sunny said they would meet me there. Annabelle needs to study for a social studies quiz, and Sunny wants to read up on spells.

Annabelle and Sunny are already in the library when I arrive. They both smile and wave me over to their table.

"I keep messing up my incantations," Sunny wails, but quietly because this is the library after all.

(An incantation, in case you didn't know, is the words you have to say out loud in a magic spell.)

Annabelle pats Sunny's back soothingly. "It just takes a little practice," she says. "I know you're going to get it, Sunny!"

I agree. "Sometimes it helps me remember if I make the words rhyme a little bit," I tell her.

Sunny looks surprised. "I can do that?" she asks. "Make the words rhyme? I thought I couldn't change them at all!"

I nod. "As long as the meaning stays exactly the same, you can change the words a little bit. It's right there in chapter one of our spells book."

Sunny smacks her forehead. "How could I have forgotten that? I think that will help me a lot. Thanks, Heidi!"

"And speaking of poems . . . ," I say. "I still have to pick an emotion for my sense poem. Maybe love?"

Both Sunny and Annabelle groan. "Enough with your crush already!" Annabelle says. "Can't you write about something else?"

"Well . . ." I hesitate. What else can I write about? "Things have been so confusing lately," I say.

"Write about that!" Sunny suggests. "Write about what confusion is like."

"Confusion . . . looks like wiggly worms," I begin.

"Ew!" Sunny and Annabelle say together.

I laugh. "Okay, how about wiggly spaghetti instead?"

"Much better," Sunny says approvingly.

"I love spaghetti!" Annabelle says.

Annabelle and Sunny return to their work, and I keep thinking.

What would confusion taste like? I wonder. *It should be a bunch of different things.*

It tastes like sweet-and-sour candy.

It smells like when my mom sprays on too much perfume.

It sounds like an alarm clock buzzing.

It feels like an itchy sweater.

It makes me anxious.

It isn't the happiest poem, I think. *But it's kind of what I am feeling right now. I just cannot write a happy poem when I'm not feeling it!*

After Sunny, Annabelle, and I finish our work and go our separate ways, I decide to see what Hunter is up to. Maybe it's not the coolest thing in the world, but it would be great to bump into Hunter any way I can, and if that means waiting by the window in the lobby of my dorm, watching for Hunter to walk by on his way to the Barn for dinner, then so be it.

My plan is to casually skip down the front steps and be like, *Wow, Hunter, fancy seeing YOU here!* Then we can walk to dinner together and maybe even sit next to each other.

I'm surprised Melanie hasn't thought of this. Following him isn't exactly flirting, but it *is* a tactic.

Eee! Here comes Hunter now!

Remember, Heidi, act normal!

I barrel out the door and skippity-hop down the steps like the most un-hung-up, carefree girl in the world. *That's ME!*

Then I watch a bunch of other boys catch up to Hunter. *Oh no!* Now he's walking with *THEM!* I fade to a safe distance.

One word: *uncool!*

As I walk behind the boys, I check out Hunter's outfit. He must have changed after dripping ice cream onto his shirt earlier.

How come when I do something like that I look like a total mess, but when Hunter does it, he makes it look like the most adorable thing to ever happen in the world?

He's wearing dark gray jersey-knit shorts and a long-sleeved cream-colored Henley shirt. I don't think I've ever seen him wear long pants. I wonder what he's going to do when it starts to get cold.

I follow the boys to the Barn, but they don't go in the main door. They enter a *side* door.

Interesting.

I follow them inside. It's a long hallway, and it looks like it turns toward the cafeteria at the other end. I wait for the boys to turn the corner.

Then I hear Hunter's voice.

"Hey! I left my backpack by the picnic tables!" he says. "Be right back."

Oh no! Hunter is HEADED this way!

I panic and look for a place to hide. The only thing in the hallway is a vending machine. I run and press myself against the wall beside the vending machine. I try to make myself as hidden as possible standing right up against the machine. I grab on to a metal bar behind the vending machine to hold myself in place.

But as soon as I pull on the metal bar, it moves toward me, like I triggered a lever, and the vending machine slides away from me.

Whoa!

I fall backward into an opening in the wall.

Then the vending machine slides back into place.

Clunk!

I hear Hunter's sneakers slap the floor as he runs by.

Whoa, where am I? I wonder as I scramble to my feet. I see some natural light coming from above.

I'm standing inside an old stairwell!

I have to find out what's up the stairs! The splintery wood creaks as I climb. The stairs turn and I go up another flight, and then another. When I get to the top, I gasp.

Oh! My! Gosh!

It's a HAYLOFT!

It must be part of the original barn from the 1800s!

The floor is still covered in hay, and there are some undisturbed hay bales stacked like pillows of giant shredded wheat against one wall. There's even a hay bale chute in one corner, and four cow-milking stools on the floor.

I breathe in the warm musty smell of the hayloft. It feels like I've stepped back in time!

I *have* to show this place to Sunny and Annabelle.

Maybe we can use it as a secret hideout to hold meetings and have private conversations! No more whispering about crushes and roommates.

It's perfect!

I creak back down the wooden stairs. **I hope I can get the vending machine to slide over again!**

In the dim light I spy the lever and pull on it. Again the vending machine slides to one side. I step into the hall, and the vending machine rolls back into place. There's nobody around so I dash down the hall to the cafeteria.

Hunter is sitting with Isabelle, Melanie, and Tate again. *That's what I get for being late.* But it's okay. **I can't wait to share my discovery with Sunny and Annabelle.**

"Hey, Heidi!" Sunny says. "Come get some tacos with us!"

I follow Sunny and Annabelle to the taco bar. I pick up a taco shell and fill it. "You are NOT going to believe the secret I've just uncovered."

Sunny sprinkles lettuce onto her taco and hands the tongs to Annabelle. They lean in closer.

"WHAT secret?!" Sunny asks.

I look around to make sure nobody's listening. "I have to show you because you won't believe it unless you see it. It's SO cool!"

Sunny and Annabelle look at each other and then back at me.

"Can you show us after dinner?" Sunny asks.

I nod as I fill a second taco shell. "Let's wait until everyone's gone, and then I'll take you there."

We finish our tacos and wait for everyone else to leave the table. I wish I could follow Hunter, but right now the secret room is more important.

My friends follow me down the long hallway. I stop in front of the vending machine.

"Are we stopping for snacks?" Sunny asks.

I shake my head.

"Nope. Watch this."

I push my back against the wall and slide my arm behind the vending machine. I find the secret lever and pull on it. The vending machine rolls aside like it did before.

My friends gasp.

"Hurry," I say, ushering them in. The vending machine slides shut behind us.

I start to walk up the stairs. "Just follow me."

When we get to the top of the stairs, I jump onto a hay bale and stretch my arms over my head, like *Ta-da!* "So what do you think?"

Sunny and Annabelle look around in wonder.

"This place is SO cool, Heidi!" Annabelle says.

Sunny perches on a milking stool. "It's udder-ly amazing!"

We all giggle.

"How did you find it?" asks Annabelle.

I tell them about following Hunter and how I almost got caught. "I hid by the vending machine, and that's when I accidentally triggered the lever and stumbled onto the secret hayloft."

Sunny shakes her head. "You're wild, Heidi Heckelbeck. And I LOVE it!"

I smile slyly. "The best part is that now we have a secret place to hold *private conversations*. It's our Secret Loft! What do you think?"

Sunny and Annabelle each slap me a high five.

"Let's have our first private conversation *right now*!" I say. "We can start with what's going on with my CRUSH!"

I lean in close to Sunny and Annabelle, but I don't whisper. I don't have to. "It seems like forever ago, but this morning I saw the *inside* of Hunter's room!"

My friends' mouths drop open. "NO WAY!" Annabelle half shouts.

I nod. "Yup, and Melanie saw it too. We used the dance flyers as an excuse to go to Hunter's dorm, and then we were talking to Hunter outside his room!"

"*Well*, what's his room like?" Annabelle asks.

I picture Hunter's room in my mind. "It's totally amazing, like he is! It has a baseball and California theme. He also has the CUTEST teddy bear on his pillow, named Bear-Z. So now I know more about him.

"Oh! Plus, in class today I also learned that he likes *LONG* hair."

Annabelle tilts her head to one side.

"What's so great about that?"

My eyes bug out. "Is that *all* you can say, Annabelle? I call this *valuable* information!"

Sunny raises an eyebrow. "But, Heidi, your hair isn't long or short—so why does it matter?"

I throw my hands into the air in frustration.

"Come on. *Keep up!* I'm going to find a spell for gorgeous long hair!"

Annabelle slants her eyebrows.

"Seriously, Heidi? A spell for long hair?"

I roll my eyes. "What's so bad about that? And maybe I can talk to him about baseball, too."

Sunny leans on the hay bale beside me. "And what do you know about baseball, Heidi?"

"I played it once," I say. "And I actually hit the ball well. I hit a home run!"

"Really?" Annabelle says. "That's great!"

"But then I ran the bases the wrong way and it didn't count," I admit.

I sigh, because all my ideas are getting shot down. "But maybe there's a spell called Learn Everything There Is to Know about Baseball in Five Minutes?"

My friends laugh.

"Or maybe there's a spell that can make me a baseball star!" I suggest.

Annabelle frowns. "Heidi, stop thinking so much about what Hunter likes and ask yourself, what does Hunter like about YOU?"

My shoulders droop. "Probably nothing."

Sunny gives me an earnest look. "Heidi, you're one of the most fun people I know! Let Hunter get to know the *real* you!"

I stare at my sneakers. "You don't get it," I say. "Isabelle and Melanie are already after Hunter, and maybe Sophie, too.

"If I don't do something drastic, he'll NEVER notice me!"

Annabelle pats my knee. "Witchcraft isn't the answer to everything, Heidi. **Remember, you're wonderful just the way you are.**"

That's easy for her to say, but if I'm so wonderful, then why doesn't Hunter want to go out with me?

And I mean, me alone.

I invited him out for ice cream, and he said yes—but then invited a bunch of other kids too.

And let's be real: **What's the point of being a witch if you can't use a little magic to help you?**

I've already stooped to following Hunter around. But I haven't stooped to magic . . .

yet.

BUBBLE, BUBBLE! POTION TROUBLE!

The time has finally come for drastic measures.

If I'm going to win over Hunter, then I have to be bold.

Why is it that when you're crazy about someone, it makes *you* act a little crazy too? I wonder if Melanie feels the same way.

Tonight we're working on our spells and potions homework in our room.

Melanie is making a love potion.

"This potion will make Hunter attracted **only to me**," she brags. "Not Isabelle. Or anyone else— **just ME**."

I want to cover my ears because I can't stand to hear this. **Melanie's words feel like daggers in my heart.**

I know she's not *trying* to be mean, because she still has no idea I like Hunter too.

I rally and put on a good show. "A *love* potion is a great idea, Melanie! And since you're an expert in potions, I'm sure you won't attract flies or mosquitoes by accident."

Melanie laughs. "You are *so* weird sometimes, Heidi."

I grin. "It's part of my charm."

But secretly I'm already scheming about how to mess up her potion.

I'll have to wait till she makes it first, of course. So for now I'll look for a spell for long hair.

I open my *Elementary Spells and Potions* booklet and return to the chapter "Potions of Attraction, Beauty, and Love."

I find potions for Soft Dewy Skin, Magnificent Makeup, Pleasant Perfumes, and then this one: Luscious Locks.

Bingo! This sounds promising!

I skim the section. It has potions for dry hair, oily hair, split ends, trendy hairstyles; and then I find just the one: Magical Hair Growth.

Let's GO!

I read over the potion.

Magical Hair Growth

This simple potion will make your locks long, luscious, and oh so silky! Simply mix the ingredients together, wash your hair as normal, and apply the potion. Chant the following spell.

Ingredients
4 strands of your hair
3 full teaspoons baby oil
5 chocolate chips, crushed
2 pinches of salt

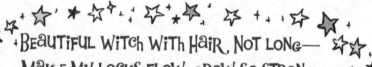

BEAUTIFUL WITCH WITH HAIR, NOT LONG—
MAKE MY LOCKS FLOW, GROW SO STRONG.
APPLY THIS POTION TO A WET HEAD OF HAIR,
THEN WATCH ALL MY FRIENDS SMILE AND STARE.

To reverse the spell, close your eyes, place your hands on top of your head, and chant the following.

HURRY! HURRY! GIVE ME STRENGTH!
MAKE MY HAIR, ITS NORMAL LENGTH!

Note: When your hair is the perfect length, twirl and do a hop. Spell lasts up to nine hours!

I actually have all the ingredients!

I scoot to the bathroom and grab baby oil, and then I go into my top desk drawer and pick out a couple of salt packets I took from the cafeteria in case I ever needed them.

I also grab some chocolate chip cookies on my dresser from lunch. I carefully pluck out five chips from the cookies, place them on a paper plate, and smoosh them with my thumb.

I stop and look over Melanie's shoulder to see how her potion is going. She has everything laid out on her desk. Her desktop is lit with battery-operated tea lights that glow and flicker.

Three words: *Cool and witchy.*

"How's it going?" I ask as I study her potion ingredients.

She has a dish of rose petals, a bear-shaped jar of honey, a cinnamon stick, rose tea, pink glitter, and

a piece of paper with Hunter's name on it. There's also an empty heart-shaped perfume bottle, and a funnel to transfer the potion into the bottle.

Melanie looks up. "All I have to do now is mix the ingredients and chant the spell. Then I'll spray myself with potion in the morning. And *voila*! Hunter will find me IRRESISTIBLE!"

Ugh, I think.

"How lucky!" I say out loud.

And I'm not lying, because it is pretty lucky to have a crush on someone and simply find a spell that will make you irresistible to him. I watch as Melanie adds honey drops to her potion with an eyedropper. Melanie inserts the funnel into the top of her perfume bottle and pours in the pink potion.

"Ta-da!" she sings. "My potion is all finished! It just needs to rest before I put the pump on top." She gets up, heads to the bathroom, and turns on the shower.

This is my chance to mess up her potion.

It's now or never!

I bite my thumbnail as my conscience kicks in. It says, *This is so mean, Heidi!*

But the other side of my brain argues back. *But Melanie will never know! She'll just think she messed up her potion. Go for it, Heidi! Do you want Hunter to notice HER or YOU?!* Correct answer: *ME.*

I look around the room for an ingredient to add to her potion.

Then I see it. Pink nail polish.

I grab the little bottle, pull out the brush, and add a drop of nail polish to Melanie's love potion. The only problem is, I can see the drop. I dig a toothpick from my tub of Thingamajiggy and Whatnots and stir the nail polish into her potion. Now it blends in perfectly.

Phew!

The shower switches off. I race to my side of the room and wrap the toothpick in a tissue. I have to get rid of the evidence! I run down the hall and drop it into the trash bin in the laundry room.

When I get back to our room, I feel wired and, not surprisingly, a little bit guilty. But I shove these thoughts aside and get to work on my potion.

There should only be two things on my mind right now: *Long hair* and *Hunter McCutie.*

I take a deep breath.

Focus, Heidi! Focus!

I mix my potion.

Poof!

It turns into a beautiful satiny hair serum. I'll chant the spell in the morning just before I use it.

Eeeee! I am SO excited! Hunter is going to LOVE my long luxurious locks!

I get ready for bed and crawl under the covers with a slightly wicked grin on my face. Things are about to get *real* with my McCutie pie!

But have I gone too far . . . ?

Six words: *Absolutely not! I'm just getting started!*

HAIR WE GO!

Time for my new hairdo! I think when my eyes pop open the next morning.

I can hardly wait to get this hair-growth spell underway.

Melanie is chanting her love potion spell right now, but **unfortunately** for her, it's not going to work.

Don't feel bad! I tell myself.

You're just competitive, and there's nothing wrong with that.

Three words: *Go, Team Heidi!*

I wait for Melanie to finish her chant before I get up.

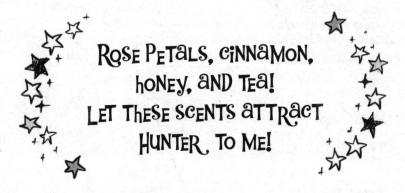

ROSE PETALS, CINNAMON, honey, AND TEA! LET THESE SCENTS ATTRACT HUNTER, TO ME!

She spritzes perfume onto her neck and wrists.

"See you in the cafeteria!" Melanie sings on her way out the door. "I'll be the one sitting next to *you know who*!"

The door clicks shut, and the smell of rose petals lingers in the room.

Okay, now it's *my* turn to get ready!

I lay out one of my favorite outfits—

a black denim skirt,

white top with lace around the collar,

and my signature black-and white- striped tights.

I shower and wash my hair. Then I comb the potion through my hair and chant the spell.

Oooh! My scalp tingles!

It must be working!

Then I slip on my outfit and stand in front of the mirror.

I tie a gray cardigan and around my shoulders, and then I run back to the mirror.

Two words: *Nailed it.*

But I do a double take when I see my hair.

OMGosh!

It's already grown *past* my shoulders.

Wow!

And it's salon perfect!

No need to dry, style, or brush it!

I flick my gorgeous long hair with the back of my hand.

I love it.

Hunter is going to *love* it.

Eeee!

I swing my backpack over my shoulder and run all the way to the cafeteria.

I've never felt SO glamorous!

Heads turn when I walk into the cafeteria.

I feel like a movie star!

I sashay to the cereal station, sprinkle cinnamon cereal into a bowl, and top it with milk.

Then I tilt my head back slightly so my hair can swing more freely. I go *swish, swish, swish* all the way to my table.

I swish right by Hunter, who's sitting with Isabelle, Melanie, and Tate again.

All eyes are on *me*, including Hunter's.

"Wow, Heidi!" Hunter says. "You look so . . ." He pauses, trying to find the right word, and I wait patiently for a mind-blowing compliment. "You look so . . . *so different* today. Did you do something to your hair?"

Okay, that wasn't exactly the compliment I was expecting, but at least he noticed! I blush and fling my long hair over one shoulder.

"It's a new style. Do you like it, Hunter?"

And before he can answer, Melanie butts in. "You look like you're trying to be Ariel from *The Little Mermaid*!"

Well, no offense to Ariel, but that comment felt like a put-down.

I laugh it off since I have no other comeback, which is Flirting Tactic Number 5, minus the head toss. Then I walk to the other side of the table and sit with Sunny and Annabelle.

"Your hair looks absolutely AMAZING," Sunny says.

I grin BIG, because that's more the reaction I was going for!

"It looks like you just did a photo shoot for a hair commercial!" Annabelle adds.

I set down my cereal. "Thanks." Then I whisper, "But do you think *Hunter* likes it?"

They both turn their heads and look at Hunter. My face heats up.

"STOP!" I whisper loudly. "Don't be so OBVIOUS!"

Sunny looks back at me. "How could he *not* like it, Heidi?" she whispers. "It looks great, but don't you want him to like you for *more* than your hair?"

I spoon some cereal. "Well, of course I do! This is just a way to get him to notice me! *Duh.*"

Sunny and Annabelle roll their eyes and change the subject to costume ideas for the dance.

"Why don't you go as a sunflower?" Annabelle suggests to Sunny. "That would be such a cute costume and perfect for you!"

"That's a good idea," Sunny agrees. "But maybe
I should stay away from 'sunny' anything for
the party, you know? I mean Halloween is
my chance to be something different.
Maybe I should go as a raindrop!" Annabelle and
Sunny both giggle.

"I want to go as something scary, but not too scary," Annabelle says. "All I can think of right now is a witch, but that's not very unique or creative . . . **especially for me because I am a witch!**"

"Let's keep thinking. I'm sure we will all come up with something," Sunny says.

I only half listen because I'm trying to figure out if Melanie's love potion is working or not.

I don't think it is, because Hunter is talking to Isabelle and Tate way more than to Melanie.

Well, at least THAT worked!

Annabelle taps my arm and snaps me out of my thoughts. "Earth to Heidi!"

I look at my friends. "What?"

Annabelle shakes her head. "Never mind. Your head is too far in the clouds to bother."

I shrug, and I'm about to go back to my cereal when Sunny wrinkles her brow.

"Now what?" I ask.

Sunny points at my hair.

"Um, Heidi? I think your hair is getting *longer*. . . ."

I look down at my hair. "Do you mean longer than when I *got* here?"

Sunny nods, and Annabelle's eyes grow wide.

"It IS getting longer, Heidi!"
Annabelle says.

I grab my hair into a ponytail. It does feel like I have a LOT more hair. "Well, maybe it's not quite finished growing yet?" I say hopefully. But something's definitely wrong. My scalp feels super prickly.

Eek. And my palms feel clammy.

Sunny leans back in her chair and checks on my hair. "Heidi, your hair is all the way down to your WAIST!"

Now everyone at our table, and at all the tables around us, is staring at me—and not in a good way.

"Look at Heidi's hair!" somebody shouts.

I reach back and twirl— make that *haul*—my hair into a huge bun.

Annabelle shoves a baseball cap in front of me. She always carries a cap with her in case it rains, because she hates umbrellas. "Here, put this on!"

I take the hat and scrunch it on top of my bun. I stuff the loose hair inside, like it's a shower cap.

Now the whole cafeteria is staring at me.

Mrs. Kettledrum sees that things have gotten a little *hairy*, and she power walks to our table. She bends over and whispers, "Heidi, please go to your room and reverse the spell. I'll put a memory-erasing spell on all the non-magical students."

As she talks, I can feel the baseball cap growing tighter and tighter on my head. When I stand up to leave, the baseball cap blasts off. Everyone watches the cap go UP and then DOWN.

Whack!

It lands on Hunter's pancakes.

The entire cafeteria erupts in laughter.

"Way to go, RAPUNZEL!" I hear someone shout.

This would be a good time for an invisibility spell, but, of course, I don't know one.

Merg.

And my hair is STILL growing.

Everyone is laughing and shouting, and above it all I hear somebody's thoughts coming in loud and clear. It's Melanie, and I can't believe what she's thinking!

Well, I guess I won't have to worry about Hunter liking Heidi after THIS!

WHAT?!

Melanie is worried about Hunter liking ME?!

I can't believe this, but she's probably right. Hunter wouldn't be interested in a girl who messes up spells and has her hair go haywire.

Sunny grabs me by the arm, and this stops the endless babbling in my head. "Heidi! Come on! We have to get you out of here!"

Now my hair has reached the FLOOR!

It's coiled around the leg of my chair, and as I start to walk, the chair drags along behind me. Everyone shrieks with laughter. To top it off, there's a cinnamon roll stuck in my hair too.

Six true words: *This is what stupidity looks like.*

Sunny and Annabelle pick up my hair like it's an overgrown vine, and escort me out of the cafeteria. Everyone is still laughing, and right now it stinks to be me. But as soon as we get outside into the sunshine, I feel better. At least I can't hear the crazy laughter anymore.

"Don't worry, Heidi," Sunny says. "This will blow over really fast."

I sigh loudly. "I hope so!" I say. "I just don't know what went wrong. I followed the instructions exactly!"

Annabelle shakes her head. "It doesn't take much to mess up a potion."

She can say THAT again! I think. *And THIS is what I deserve for messing with Melanie's potion!*

Sunny and Annabelle comfort me all the way to my dorm.

They say things like, "It'll be okay, Heidi."

"This stuff happens to witches all the time."

"It might make Hunter like you even more!"

I don't know about the *last* comment, but my friends make me feel better.

"Thanks so much for everything. You two are true friends. I'll catch up with you later," I say when we get to my dorm room. "Right now I have to reverse this *hair-i-fying* spell."

Sunny and Annabelle hug me. Then I drag myself and my hair into my room.

Ouch! Some of my hair shuts in the door.

I look in the mirror, and all I can think is:

Mirror, mirror on the wall, who's the hairiest of them all?

I reach for my spell booklet and reread the spell.

Now I see where I went wrong. Underneath the spell it says to do a *twirl and a hop* when your hair reaches the perfect length.

Missed *that* part. Total rookie move!

One word: *oops!*

The chant to reverse the spell is at the bottom of the page. I close my eyes, place my hands on top of my head, and chant the reversal spell.

HURRY! HURRY! GIVE ME STRENGTH!
MAKE MY HAIR ITS NORMAL LENGTH!

POOF!

My head feels instantly lighter. I run back to the mirror.

My hair is its regular, boring old length!

Woo-hoo!

I do a victory dance.

I still think this spell would've been great if I hadn't goofed it up. My mind starts scheming all over again.

I'm not about to give up on my crush THAT easily.

But for now I have to go, or I'll be late for class.

Eek!

Better late than HAIRY!

GOiNG BONKERS

Melanie brings up the hair fiasco as we walk into English class. "Heidi, you were *HAIR*-larious at breakfast this morning!"

I sigh and look the other away. "It wasn't *hair-larious* if you were ME."

Melanie laughs. "Oh, come on, Heidi. It was *hair*-sterical! It's not like you have some royal reputation to uphold, and besides, it gave everyone a good laugh."

I plunk my book bag onto an empty desk. I'm not even going to attempt to sit next to Hunter after what happened.

"But, Melanie, the laughs were at *my* expense."

Melanie bursts into more giggles, and even though I don't think she means to hurt me, I know she's happy that I made a fool of myself.

"So how'd your love potion go?" I ask with fake innocence, and also because I want to change the subject.

Melanie sits at the desk next to me—that's because Hunter is sitting at the desk next to her on the other side.

Two words: *surprise, surprise.*

"My love potion was a total flop," she whispers so Hunter can't hear. He's talking to Isabelle, so it doesn't really matter.

"I can't understand *why* it didn't work," she goes on. "But I'm going to try again." Then Melanie turns and gives me an unexpectedly fierce look.

"Heidi, by any chance did you mess with my love potion?"

I swallow uncomfortably.

"Of course not!" I say a little too defensively. "I would *never* do that!"

Melanie folds her arms against her chest. "Well, you might if you were crushing on the *same* guy."

Suddenly my brain glitches, detecting panic in the operating system. But I act cool. "Why would you say that?"

Melanie holds up four fingers. "I'll tell you why," she whispers (after first taking a quick look to make sure Hunter isn't paying attention).

Then she counts a reason on each finger.

"Number one: Hunter is ridiculously cute and everyone likes him.

"Number two: because you won't tell me your mystery crush.

"Number three: we both heard him say he likes long hair, and suddenly you turn into Rapunzel.

"And number four: my love potion didn't work, and I never screw up my potions. *That's why.*"

Whoa! When did Melanie become such a master detective!

Should I just fess up?

Probably not. It would ruin our already fragile friendship.

On the other hand, she doesn't seem *that* mad. *But don't be fooled, Heidi. You know this trick.* Melanie is pretending to be nice so you'll feel safe and tell her the truth. *Only, once you tell her, she'll go ballistic.*

Conclusion: lie to protect both of us.

"Are you KIDDING?" I say, pretending to be shocked. "Hunter is *not* my mystery crush, and the only reason I can't tell you *who* I like is because I want to know if he likes me back *first*." The last part is actually *true*. The first part is, of course, a whopping big lie.

Oh help! When did I become so devious?

Melanie harumphs. And since class is starting, she thankfully lets go of it . . . *for now*.

Our teacher, Ms. Langley, begins class by gushing about our sense poems. She says we're all emotional geniuses. Then she walks around the room and passes out our poems.

I GOT AN A.

Woo!

A's are beautiful!

A's are perfection!

A's are totally rare!

I'm so happy about my A until Ms. Langley says . . .

"Now we're going to *share* your poems out loud! Let's begin with Melanie! Come to the front of the room and **share your poem with the class.**"

WHAT? I think.

SHARE OUR POEMS OUT LOUD?!

In front of the WHOLE class?

No way!

Not happening.

If there's one thing I *don't* like, it's sharing personal stuff in front of my classmates.

I can't do this!

My poem is MY personal business, and I don't want other people to see what's going on inside my head. I look at the door.

Maybe I can make a run for it?

I try to think of excuses to leave the classroom, but Ms. Langley is one of those teachers who won't even let you leave to go to the bathroom during class.

Ugh, I'm doomed.

I watch Melanie, aka **Miss Poise and Togetherness,** walk to the front. She makes it look like it's a privilege for us to hear her poem. She pulls her perfect hair into a scrunchie and then holds her paper in front of her and nods first at the teacher, **then at Hunter, and then at the whole entire class!** She reads her poem calmly and with feeling.

One word: *disgusting.*

"My emotion poem is called 'Beautiful.' Beautiful looks like a pink sunset. Beautiful tastes like pink lemonade."

A boy interrupts. "Is everything in your poem PINK?"

Melanie wrinkles her nose. "Not *everything*." Then she continues her poem—completely unruffled. **How does she do it?!**

Another word: *impressive.*

"Beautiful smells like pink cotton candy." Here she pauses and says, "Okay, that was the last pink thing. Beautiful sounds like a lullaby. It makes me feel wonderful . . . *and BEAUTY-FULL!*"

A few kids clap, and Ms. Langley thanks Melanie. Melanie smiles, **especially at Hunter,** and returns to her seat.

Uh-oh!

Now Ms. Langley is going to call on somebody else! I slink down in my seat and stare intently at my lap.

Please don't pick me! PLEASE don't pick me!

My prayer of pleading works. **She doesn't pick me!** She chooses Hunter! I sit back up because I don't want to miss a single word!

Hunter walks to the front of the classroom. He doesn't look nervous either. Meanwhile, Melanie slides the scrunchie off her ponytail. Her gorgeous blond hair tumbles down past her shoulders. She swings her head from side to side like I did this morning to get Hunter's attention.

Note to self: the hair swish should be added to *Melanie's Guide to Flirting*.

Hunter begins to read his poem, so I shush my inner dialogue.

"My poem is called 'Joyful,'" he says.

Joyful? I think. **Wow.** I didn't know boys wrote poems about being joyful. I stare at Hunter adoringly and hang on his every word.

"Joyful looks like a home run going over the wall. It smells like buttered popcorn. It sounds like a crowd cheering. It feels like a new leather baseball glove. It tastes like a hot dog with lots of mustard. It makes me feel *great*."

This time the whole class claps, including me.

But Melanie gets the prize for clapping the loudest.

I wish she would just *relax*!

I'm completely lost in thought when Ms. Langley calls on me.

Help!

Ambush!

How did I briefly forget that I might have to stand before my peers and spill my guts? My mouth feels cottony, just like it did on the first day of school.

What if I can't talk?

It's not like I need *two* embarrassing experiences in one day.

Thank goodness I didn't do my poem on *jealousy*.

Embarrassing!

But my poem isn't upbeat, like Melanie's and Hunter's. It's weird, dark, and chaotic. If my poem were a drawing, it would be a bunch of squiggles.

"Take it away, Rapunzel!" Caden shouts.

This comment unravels me even more. At least he didn't call me Hairy Heidi like I heard Tate did.

Somehow amid the mocking, the angst, and the terror, I stand up.

My hands are shaking. My legs feel wobbly.

I think I might throw up, but I make it to the front of the classroom. I look out at my classmates.

Just get it over with, Heidi. I take a deep breath and go for it.

"My poem is called 'Stress.'"

Even though Annabelle and Sunny liked my "Confusion" poem, stress felt more like how I feel these days—stressed out!

Everyone giggles, but I press on.

"Stress looks like a cat stuck in a bath."

Everyone laughs, and this makes me feel a tiny bit better.

"Stress tastes like sour milk."

"Eeeeeew!" the class shouts.

"Stress smells like stinky armpits."

The class *shrieks* with laughter. I laugh a little too.

"Stress sounds like fingernails on a chalkboard."

"Ohhhhhhh!" everyone moans.

"Stress feels like a hundred woodpeckers pecking at your head."

More big laughs.

"Stress makes me feel like I'm at the dentist. And I can't wait for it to be over."

As soon as I'm done, I race back to my seat.

Everyone cheers and claps like crazy.

What's going on? Did they *like* my poem? Does everyone secretly have stress? Maybe I'm funny?

Now I just feel bewildered. Then Hunter leans behind Melanie's chair and gives me two thumbs-up. I smile.

What a great feeling!

Maybe Hunter likes me after all!

After morning classes and lunch, I walk back to the dorms with Melanie, Hunter, and Isabelle. I wish we could walk for HOURS. It feels fun to be with all three of them—even though Isabelle and Melanie are the competition.

LOL!

Hunter pats my shoulder playfully as we walk.

"Heidi, your poem was hilarious!" he says. "I loved it!"

Melanie pats me from the other side. "Yeah, you've gone from being a first-class *goof* to being a red-carpet *celebrity* today!"

Hunter gives Melanie a funny look. He detects the snarkiness in her comment.

But my victory feeling lasts for only about two seconds.

"I loved *your* poem, too," Hunter tells Isabelle. "I feel the same way about sports!"

Isabelle wrote her poem about excitement.

"Thanks, Mush," she says.

Mush?

Why did Isabelle call him *Mush*?

"Mush" sounds like a pet name, like "Sugar Pie!"

My mind cartwheels. *Is there something actually going on between Hunter and Isabelle?*

Ugh, crushing is so exhausting!

But I have to focus on the positives. My sense poem was a hit, and I feel much better about public speaking.

Maybe I should do stand-up comedy for a living!

LOL! Not a chance!

Because I want to be the best witch in the world!!!

And I also want to be an emotionally stable witch, because being a middle school witch has a lot of ups and downs.

Six words: *Get me OFF this roller coaster!*

TALK iT UP!

Melanie and I head back to our room to redo our spells and potions assignment.

No more backfiring beauty potions!

I pull out my *Elementary Spells and Potions* booklet and flip through the pages yet again. I find a spell that's pretty cool, but kind of babyish. It's called, How to Make Your Stuffed Animal Talk.

Hmm, I have a *better* idea!

What if I make Mrs. Kettledrum's dog, Momo, TALK?! Now *that* would be cool. I might even get extra credit! And if my spell bombs, I can always use the stuffed-animal spell as a backup. I go over my backup spell first.

How to Make Your Stuffed Animal Talk

Have you ever wished your stuffed animal could talk? What questions would you ask it? What secrets would you share? Would you stay up late and have conversations under the covers? If you've always wished a stuffed animal could talk, then this is the spell for you!

Ingredients

The written alphabet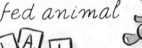
Your favorite stuffed animal
3 Scrabble tiles

Place the ingredients in a bowl. Hold your wand in your right hand and place your left hand over the mix. Tap the bowl and chant the following spell.

EAST! WEST! NORTH! SOUTH!
MAKE THIS _____ A MOTORMOUTH!
[TYPE OF STUFFED ANIMAL]

I write down the alphabet on a piece of paper, grab three tiles from my travel Scrabble board, and snag my stuffed baby seal, Snowdrop, from my bed.

I put everything into a bag in case I need it.

Now to come up with a *new* spell to make Mrs. Kettledrum's dog talk.

Eeee!

I hope this works.

I've never made up my own spell before.

I'm going to call it Talking Pets.

Next I will carefully select my ingredients.

I search through my tub of Thingamajiggy and Whatnots and pick out ingredients for my spell and list them.

INGREDIENTS

1 box of candy conversation hearts
1 page from the dictionary
1 piece of string (to loosen the tongue)
1 English Breakfast tea packet (so the pet
     will speak English)
1 page with the written alphabet
1 piece of paper with the pet's name

Finally I write directions for my spell.

Place the ingredients in a bowl, except for
the pet's name. Hold your wand in your right
hand and place your left hand over the mix.
Tap the bowl with your wand and chant the
following spell.

"If animals could talk, what would they say?
'Hi, how are you? What a beautiful day!'
Now mix these letters and words to teach.
And so give this pet, _____,
the gift of speech!"   [name of pet]

+ 199 +

"Eeee!" I squeal.

Melanie turns around. "What are *you* so giddy about?"

I spin around in my chair. "I'm excited to try my new spell!"

Melanie raises an eyebrow. "Are you going to turn yourself into a *yeti* this time?!"

She cracks herself up.

I hop off my chair and kneel in front of my tub of trinkets. "Very funny. So will you be ready to leave for class in ten?"

Melanie nods. "My love potion is all done!" She holds up the bottle of pink potion and sprays her arms and neck.

"And *this* time it's going to work! For one thing, I won't be letting it out of my sight."

She squints at me suspiciously like she knows I messed up her last potion.

It's as if she sees right through me!

I gather the rest of my ingredients while Melanie chants her spell. Then we head for the basement entrance to the School of Magic.

I can't wait to get to spells and potions class.

This time I'm actually excited to share my spell in front of the class—**even if it bombs.**

I like the magical challenge! No more beginner stuff.

When we get to class, Melanie places her hand on the chair next to her. "I'm saving this seat for Hunter."

I want to whine, *No fair-zees!* but instead I reluctantly take the seat behind her.

Then Hunter swaggers into the room.

Eeeee! He is sooooo cute!!!

Melanie whaps the free chair with her hand so Hunter will see.

Whoosh! He beelines for the empty chair.

Hunter is attracted to Melanie, like sprinkles to a doughnut.

The love potion is definitely working.

And I have a front-row seat for the show.

Melanie and Hunter volley compliments back and forth like a tennis ball.

They're *so* lovey-dovey!

Normally this would make me jealous, but I know it's *not* real.

It's only the spell.

Melanie eats up the attention anyway. And her flirting techniques are all on display: smiling, giggling, eye-batting, hair-swishing, and witty remarks.

One word: *EWW.*

Luckily, Mrs. Kettledrum and Momo soon call the class to order. She winks at me and points to her hair, which is red, like mine, but she's referring to my hair disaster, of course, not the color.

I smile and give her a thumbs-up. Then I wonder if I

should've asked permission to do an original spell, **especially one that involves *her* dog.** I'll just ask her when it's my turn to present.

Mrs. Kettledrum clasps her hands. "Welcome, budding witches and wizards! I trust you all had fun experimenting with your potions and spells!"

A positive murmur circles the room. For no reason at all Mrs. Kettledrum's dog starts looking at me and barking excitedly.

It's almost as if she knows I have a spell that involves her!

Mrs. Kettledrum hugs Momo and speaks to her soothingly. "What's the matter, Momo? My little Momo Bear? Who's the best doggie in the world? It's my Momo Baby, of course! Now, hush. Be a good girl, and let's watch everyone present their potions."

Momo's tail wags wildly at the sound of Mrs. Kettledrum's voice, and then she calms down and looks at the class expectantly.

"I know all of you may find this *hard* to believe," she continues, "but I was young once too, and I remember those exciting early days of learning to hone my magic skills. Therefore, I want to remind each of you to read and *REread* your spells and follow them *exactly*. If you don't pay close attention, you could make yourself ill or accidentally hurt one of your friends—"

"Or make your hair go *BONKERS*!" someone behind me shouts, which is followed by laughs and snickers.

"Exactly! So always be extra careful," Mrs. Kettledrum says. "Okay, now it's time to share the spells and potions you did for homework. Caleb Kim—let's start with you."

I go back to watching Melanie and Hunter. Hunter is slowly scootching his seat closer to Melanie's. And Isabelle, who's sitting on the other side of Hunter, is scooching *her* seat closer to Hunter's. Isabelle passes him a note, like she did the other day. Hunter takes it, but this time he doesn't read it. He turns his attention back to Melanie. **Isabelle kicks Hunter's foot.** He waves her off without turning his head.

Wow, this is great entertainment!
Except it kind of stinks, too, because it doesn't involve me. At least for now.

Mrs. Kettledrum taps her wand on her desk to get the class to pay attention. Poor Caleb is standing helplessly in front of the class. Mrs. Kettledrum tells him to go ahead. Caleb clears his throat.

"Well, I'm always hungry," he begins, "so I worked on food spells." He sets a lemon on Mrs. Kettledrum's desk. "I will now attempt to turn this ordinary lemon into a banana."

Caleb waves his wand over the lemon and chants the spell.

"FIDDLEDY FEE! FIDDLEDY FO-NANNA! MAKE THIS LEMON A RIPE BANANA!"

He taps his wand on the lemon, and *POOF!* It turns it into a banana. Caleb peels the banana and takes a bite to show it's real.

Some kids *oooh* and *aaah*.

Then Caleb places a carrot on the desk and tries to turn it into a chocolate bar. But it stays a carrot.

"I don't get it," he cries. "It worked this morning!"

Mrs. Kettledrum picks up the carrot. "How many times have you done this spell today, Caleb?"

Caleb thinks for a moment. "Three times."

Mrs. Kettledrum chuckles knowingly. "Your spell will work again tomorrow," she says. "The School of Magic puts limits on food spells, **or else everyone would change their chicken and spinach into candy and ice cream.**"

We all laugh. She's probably right!

Then Mrs. Kettledrum calls on Melanie. Melanie picks up her heart-shaped bottle of pink love potion and flounces to the front of the class.

And *GET THIS!*

Hunter *follows* her!!!

OMGiggles. This should be good.

Hunter stands next to Melanie.

Did he just sniff her hair?

Ew!

"Hi, everyone!" Melanie sings. "I'm Melanie Maplethorpe, and I **made a *love* potion** from the chapter 'Potions of Attraction, Beauty, and Love.'" As soon as she says "love potion," Hunter

makes a heart with his hands and pumps it in and out so it looks like a heart beating.

The class whistles and laughs, everyone except for Isabelle and me. I'm in shock, and Isabelle is scowling.

Her arms are folded tightly against her chest. Melanie and Hunter are putting on quite a show.

"To make this love potion," Melanie begins, "I simply mixed rose petals, honey, one cinnamon stick, rose tea, and pink glitter together in this beautiful perfume jar. I also wrote the name of my crush."

Here Melanie hesitates for a moment. "For this experiment I used Hunter, but that doesn't necessarily mean HE is my crush!

"Anyway, I wrote the name 'Hunter' on a small piece of paper, rolled it up, and stuck it inside the bottle. Then I tapped the bottle with my wand, sprayed my wrists and neck with the potion, and chanted the following spell:

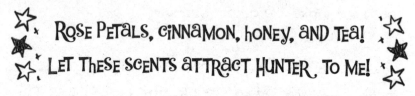

ROSE PETALS, CINNAMON, HONEY, AND TEA!
LET THESE SCENTS ATTRACT HUNTER, TO ME!

"As you can see, it worked like a charm on Hunter."

Hunter smiles and makes googly eyes at Melanie. It's as if he's in a trance. Then Hunter grabs the perfume bottle and holds it for everyone to see. "Melanie's potion is totally irresistible! And she's not even paying me to say this!"

The class bursts into laughter—even Isabelle and I laugh. But Melanie has a lot of nerve.

How could she make adorable Hunter look like a fool in front of the whole class?

It's pretty harsh.

Finally the class settles down. Mrs. Kettledrum smiles at Melanie. "Excellent work, Melanie. But I have to caution you about using spells where people's actual feelings are involved."

Then Mrs. Kettledrum turns toward my direction and calls on me next!

Eeeee! I grab my stuff and walk to the front of the room. I tap Mrs. Kettledrum on the arm. She bends down to my level.

"Is it okay if I try an original spell?" I whisper.

Mrs. Kettledrum looks at me and smiles. "How enterprising, Heidi!" she says. "I'll stay magically on guard in case anything goes wrong."

I tap her arm again. "There's one more thing. May I borrow Momo for the spell?"

Mrs. Kettledrum steps back slightly. "My—Momo? My little Momo Bear?"

I nod.

"Well, okay, Heidi, if you must."

Mrs. Kettledrum sets Momo on a chair in front of the class. I begin to speak.

"Hi, everybody! Well, you'll be happy to know I'm not doing that hairbrained spell I did earlier today!"

The class starts laughing.

"Today I'm going to attempt a spell I've never tried before—and I made it up myself!"

My classmates glance at each other with frightened looks, like they think I'm going to turn them into a bunch of frogs or something.

Lol! Maybe another day.

"I got the idea for this spell from *another* spell in our booklet. My spell is called Talking Pets.

"And don't worry, if my spell gets out of control, Mrs. Kettledrum will fix it."

Then I list the ingredients and put them into my bowl.

"Now to chant my spell!

"IF ANIMALS COULD TALK, WHAT WOULD THEY SAY?
'HI, HOW ARE YOU? WHAT A BEAUTIFUL DAY!'
NOW MIX THESE LETTERS AND WORDS TO TEACH.
AND SO GIVE THIS PET, MOMO, THE GIFT OF SPEECH!"

I tap my wand on the edge of the bowl, and sparkles swirl around Momo's head. Everybody waits expectantly.

But Momo doesn't say a word.

Hmm, maybe I should ask her something!

"Hi, Momo! I've been wondering, what do you think of Mrs. Kettledrum?"

Momo looks affectionately at Mrs. Kettledrum and barks.

Disappointing, I think, and I'm about to give up when Momo answers in English.

"I love her with all my heart!"

Mrs. Kettledrum puts her hand over her heart, and her eyes get teary.

Everyone else stands up and claps!

Mrs. Kettledrum pats Momo on the head. "Well, that's the nicest thing I've ever heard!" she says, reaching for her handkerchief.

"I love you too, Momo, more than anything else in the world."

The class cheers and whistles.

When everyone settles down, I ask another question. "Momo, do you like coming to class?"

Momo yips sharply. "I love coming to class!" she says. "It's my favorite part of the day!"

More cheers and roars from the class. Wow, I can't believe this!

My spell actually WORKED!

I've never felt so accomplished in my entire life.

It's epic!

I ask Momo more questions. My final one is: "Momo, Mrs. Kettledrum has lots of cute nicknames for you. Momo Bear, Momo Baby, Momo Missy. What's your nickname for Mrs. Kettledrum?"

Momo hops off the chair and trots into Mrs. Kettledrum's outstretched arms. "I like to call her Mrs. CUDDLE-drum!" Momo says, licking our teacher on the cheek.

"*Awwwwww,*" the whole class says, including me.

One word: *adorable.*

When I'm done, Mrs. Kettledrum—who's still holding Momo—walks over to me. "Heidi, that was outstanding.

"A-plus-plus-*PLUS*!"

Momo barks. "Thank you, Heidi," Momo says. "Those are things I've wanted to say my whole life."

The entire class stands and claps for me again.

Wow, how can the worst day of my life turn into the best day ever?

I get cheers and high fives all the way back to my table. I'm pretty sure I'm glowing from head to toe.

Melanie turns around in her seat. "That was amazing, Heidi," she says. "You really surprise me sometimes."

I smile at Melanie and feel really happy.

If only we could be friends like this all the time, I think.

Melanie turns back around before I can say anything. Then I notice that Hunter is talking to Isabelle now. Looks like the love potion wore off.

Poor Melanie.

The presentations continue with other students showing off their spells. It is so much fun!

At the end of the class, Mrs. Kettledrum claps to get our attention again. "Okay, everybody—that will be all the spells and potions we'll share for today. Does anyone have any questions?"

A girl named Ava O'Connor raises her hand. She has long wavy brown hair, and she's super-shy. Mrs. Kettledrum calls on her.

"I'm having trouble with my spells," Ava says. "I get really nervous and my spells never seem to work. What should I do?"

I hold my hand straight up.

I know the answer to this problem!

Mrs. Kettledrum points to me.

"You can't be scared when you cast a spell or it won't work. If you're calm and confident, your spells will work every time."

Mrs. Kettledrum smiles broadly. "That's exactly right, Heidi. Did your mom or aunt teach you that?"

I shake my head. "Neither. I learned it through trial and error. When I approach my spells with excitement and confidence, they're always successful. That is, if I remember to read ALL the directions."

Mrs. Kettledrum *loves* my answer.

She turns to Ava. "Now, Ava, I suggest you start with simple spells, like making a book fly across an empty room. Then ask yourself, what's the worst thing that can happen if I fail? Maybe the book doesn't move or it crashes onto the floor. Soon you'll find there's nothing to worry about and your spells will become more and more successful."

Ava nods. "Thank you, Mrs. Kettledrum and Heidi. I'll try that next time."

Brrrrrrrring!

The bell rings and everyone scrambles to get going. Kids walk past me and praise my Talking Pets spell, and Ava thanks me for my advice.

"Coolest spell EVER, Heidi," Hunter says on his way out.

Wow, I think. *I knocked it out of the park today!*

Maybe THIS will make Hunter fall for me!

I swing my backpack over my shoulder.

"Heidi," Mrs. Kettledrum calls, "may I speak with you for a moment?"

I walk back to the front of the room. Momo licks my ankles. She's not talking anymore, but I know exactly what she's saying. *Thank you!*

I stoop down and pet her between the ears.

"Heidi, that was a wonderful demonstration of magic today. You're an exceptional student—both intuitive and fearless. I'm *very* impressed. Would you like to work with me privately on furthering your magic skills?"

My mouth falls open.

"Would I ever!"

Momo barks her approval too.

"Good!" Mrs. Kettledrum says. "I'll look at my schedule, and then we can set something up."

I nod.

"That would be amazing. *Thank you!!!*"

I skip all the way out the door. I can't wait to tell Sunny and Annabelle my news!

And I'll bet Hunter will find me irresistible now!

Well, at least I hope so.

ARE YOU MAD?

Wump!

I plunk onto the seat across from Sunny and Annabelle at dinner. **Somehow I *never* get to the cafeteria in time to sit next to Hunter.**

Merg.

But I'm actually too excited to care right now. Plus, I have another plan in mind for dinner.

"Pssssst!" I hiss at Sunny and Annabelle from across the table. "Let's get sandwiches and take them to the Loft. **I have BIG news!**"

Sunny and Annabelle push out their chairs at the same time.

We race to the sandwich bar. When it's warm weather, we're allowed to take sandwiches to the picnic tables outside—*or* sneak up to our secret room!

Hee-hee!

We pack sammies, chips, bottled waters, and cookies in brown bags. Then we casually walk to the vending machine in the hallway, aka the entrance to the Secret Loft.

I open the hidden door, and we stampede up the stairs. Then we hop onto the hay bales and break out our food.

"So what's your BIG news, Heidi?" Sunny asks.

I unwrap my turkey-cranberry sandwich and lay it on the wrapper.

"Well, you're *not* going to believe this!" I say, tearing into my chips.

"But today I invented my *own* spell and performed it in front of my spells and potions class—and it WORKED!" I tell them.

Annabelle drops the cap from her water bottle, and it falls onto the hay. "Wow, Heidi! That's brilliant! What was your spell?"

I reach down, grab the cap, and hand it back to Annabelle. "It was SO cool!

"I actually made Mrs. Kettledrum's dog, Momo, *TALK*!"

Sunny and Annabelle stop eating.

I open and close my fingers, like I'm operating a puppet.

"Yup, Momo the Talking Dog!

"And I asked Momo questions, and she answered them in perfect English." I say proudly.

Annabelle sets her sandwich down. "Whoa, you *actually* made a dog TALK? Heidi, that is so *advanced!*"

I blush. "Well, I had no idea if my spell would work, but it DID!"

Sunny stuffs potato chips into her sandwich.

"Good for you, Heidi," she says, but the tone of her voice makes it sound like she's *not* that happy for me.

Weird.

I swig my water and ignore the strange vibe.

"And the whole class gave me a standing ovation!

"Today I went from a first-class mess, after my scary-hairy spell, to a superstar!"

Annabelle laughs and flings a chip at me.

"That's awesome, Heidi. You sure didn't let the bad-hair spell get you down!" she says.

I smile and hold my hand up, like, *STOP!* Because I haven't even shared my BIGGEST news.

"And here's the best part. After class Mrs. Kettledrum called me an *exceptional* student and asked me if I wanted *private* lessons with her!

"Isn't that great?!"

Annabelle claps her hands. "Heidi, that's a-*may*-zing!"

I look at Sunny for a reaction, but she's still acting weirdly quiet. "Is everything okay, Sunny?"

Sunny half smiles. "I'm fine, Heidi. And yup, that's great news."

Annabelle and I exchange a look like, *What's up with her?*

"Okay, new topic!" I say, trying to lighten the mood. "I want to thank you both again for helping me during my hair disaster! I figured out how I flubbed up the spell."

Annabelle laughs, but not Sunny.

"Your hair was like three horse tails combined!" Annabelle says.

I grab a fistful of hair and start neighing like a horse. "*Neeeiiiigh!* It gives new meaning to the expression 'having a bad hair day,'"

I say, and then I blab on about reading our sense poems aloud in class, and, of course, I tell them about Melanie's love potion and how Hunter fell all over her for a hot minute.

Annabelle giggles. "After *your* hair fiasco and Melanie's *ridiculous* love potion, **are you going to promise to *stop* trying to attract Hunter?**"

I grin like a fairy-tale fox.

"Of course I'm not going to promise that, Annabelle! I *WANT* Hunter to notice me! *Duh.*"

Sunny suddenly—and aggressively—wraps up her half-eaten sandwich.

"No offense, Heidi, but you're going too far," she says. "You have this crush thing all wrong. **If you want Hunter to like you, just be *yourself*.**"

I narrow my eyes at Sunny. Why is she so annoyed with me?

Then Annabelle chimes in. "Sunny is right. Being yourself is *always* a good idea," she says.

"You can also show interest in Hunter by asking him about baseball. Or what it was like to grow up in California. You can even tell him you liked his sense poem," Annabelle continues.

I lean back on a hay bale. "Yeah, right! Can you imagine me just randomly walking up to Hunter and saying, 'Hey, Hunter! Loved your poem!' You have to admit, that sounds pretty dorky."

Sunny tosses her hair and doesn't look at me. "Compliments are NOT dorky."

Okay, now I *know* Sunny is mad at me.

I tread carefully.

"You're right, Sunny. Compliments are *not* dorky," I say, mostly to be agreeable.

I change the topic again—only this time to **get it off me!**

"So have you both thought more about your costumes for the dance yet?"

Annabelle stuffs her trash into her brown bag. "I really want to go as something scary, but I just can't think of the perfect thing. So maybe I could go as a heart-shaped box of chocolates, but I'm not sure I'd be able to dance," she says.

I laugh. "But it would be a great costume for photo ops! What about you, Sunny?"

Sunny sighs.

It seems like it's an effort for her to even talk to me.

"I haven't thought much about it since I've been so focused on my magic classes. Maybe I'll just dress in a simple costume. Like a cat."

"But that's so boring," I say before I even think about how that might sound.

Sunny gives me a hurt look.

"Hey, what if we all dressed up as a theme?" Annabelle suggests. "We could go as a sun, a rainbow, and maybe rain—or a pot of gold?!"

I roll my eyes. "Ha-ha-ha! Yeah, right. I can just imagine Hunter saying, 'Heidi you're the cutest little pot of gold I've ever seen!' There's got to be a better costume for me!"

Annabelle frowns.

Oops, now I've just insulted Annabelle's idea.

My friends begin to pack up their stuff.

Suddenly I feel like *Heidi Hurtful.*

We leave our Secret Loft in silence. As we part ways, I hear Sunny say something to me in her thoughts.

Heidi, I know you're going to plan something to attract Hunter, but PLEASE be careful.

I turn around and look at Sunny.

"Don't worry, Sunny! I'm not going to do anything *stupid,* if that's what you mean!" Then I walk off, because I'm tired of Sunny's sour-faced mood, and now she's made *me* mad.

And even though I'm mad, I also feel really bad. On the way back to my dorm, I realize two things.

One: *I've been talking about myself way too much.*

And two: *my friends are probably sick of hearing about my crush on Hunter.*

Okay, I get it.

I walk into my room and throw my backpack onto my bed.

What a day! I'm totally pooped.

I feel Melanie's eyes on me. She's propped against the cream pillows on her bed.

"Well, well, it looks like Rapunzel has returned to her tower!" she says, but in a teasing, not mean way. It's refreshing.

She lays her book on the bed. "That spell you did on Momo today was unbelievably cool, Heidi. Would you please write it down for me? I've *always* wanted to know what my pug, Lola, is thinking."

I hop onto my bed and sink into the pillows.

I can't believe Melanie actually finds something about me cool.

One word: *rare.*

"Sure!" I say.

Melanie grabs one of her pillows and hugs it. "Oh yay! So, what did you think of my love potion spell?"

I grab a couple of books off my bedside table. "Your potion was like a love magnet, Melanie! Hunter couldn't leave your side."

Her face lights up. "It was so amazing to have Hunter's full attention—even if it only lasted a few minutes. Do you think he likes me?"

I shrug. "Who knows? Hunter is so nice to EVERYONE—it's hard to say."

Melanie pulls off her scrunchie and redoes her ponytail. "You're right! He *is* nice to everyone— *even you*!"

The way she says this makes me feel like I'm gum on the bottom of Hunter's shoe, but I don't think Melanie meant it that way—or did she?

We are competing for the same guy, even if she doesn't totally know it.

"Do you think I should keep chasing him, or is it a lost cause?" Melanie asks.

I open my spell book to the table of contents. "It's definitely not a lost cause," I say, but I'm saying this more to myself than to Melanie.

She leans back against her pillows and sighs dreamily. "I totally agree."

Melanie goes back to reading, and I open up a new book I found in the library, called *Potent Potions*. I study the chapter headings. I'm not exactly sure what I'm looking for, but I'll know it when I see it.

And that's when I see it.

The *perfect* spell.

It's called Love and Isolation. The spell isolates your crush from all the competition!

And *this* spell won't wear off until I choose to undo it.

Eeee!

I finally found my ticket to love!

Now I'll have Hunter McCutie all to myself.

Three words: *Mine, all MINE!*

11

PRiNCE CHARM-iNG!

The next day after classes, I read over the Love and Isolation spell.

Love and Isolation

Do you have a crush on someone? Would you like to get your crush's attention—and keep it? Is your crush the kind of person who's nice to everyone and you never know where you stand? If you want to know if your crush likes you back, then it is time to isolate your crush and find out once and for all!

INGREDIENTS

1 piece of paper with your crush's name written on it
1 gift for your crush
1 empty cup
1 thing unwanted
1 howl of a lone wolf

INSTRUCTIONS

1. Gather the first four ingredients into a bowl.
2. Hold one hand over the mix.
3. With your wand in your other hand, howl like a lone wolf and then chant the following spell.

_____, _____, that's my love!
[name of person two times]

Fly to my side just like a dove.

Say goodbye to all your friends.

Later on we'll make amends.

Now all your fans are off the shelf.

I have _____ to myself!
[name of same person]

It's time for me to dominate!

One, two, three, four, ISOLATE!

I have everything except a gift for Hunter. I make a dash for the door.

Melanie looks up from her homework. "Hey, where are you going?"

I twist the doorknob. "The bookstore. Need anything?"

Melanie nods. "A pack of sour gummies?"

I open the door. "Got it!"

I run all the way to the campus bookstore, which is in the Barn. I scan the shelves for a gift for Hunter.

He probably has a ton of school logo stuff.

I walk over to the gift section. They have stationery, stuffed animals, stickers, travel-size games, animal erasers, and—*ooh!* backpack charms!

I spy a baseball-glove charm and pluck it from the rack. I also grab a bag of sour gummy worms.

I pay for my stuff and zoom back to my dorm. Melanie is gone, but she left a note.

At the library.
Be back in an hour.
　　　　—Mel

Perfect! Now I can cast my spell *in private.*

I set my bowl on the bathroom counter. Then I scribble Hunter's name on a piece of paper and drop it in. I add the backpack charm and a plastic cup. Then I fish a rotten banana peel from the wastebasket for something *unwanted,* and add it to the mix.

One word: *gross!*

Time for some magic!

I place one hand over the mix. Grab my wand with my other hand.

Ready or not! Here goes!

I howl like a wolf and chant the spell.

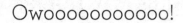

Owoooooooooooo!
Hunter, Hunter, that's my love!
Fly to my side just like a dove.
Say goodbye to all your friends.
Later on we'll make amends.
Now all your fans are off the shelf.
I have Hunter to myself!
It's time for me to dominate.
One, two, three, four, ISOLATE!

The bowl sizzles, and the backpack charm begins to glow.

Eeee!

The spell has activated!

Now all I have to do is give Hunter his gift! I pull the charm from the bowl and zip it inside a pouch in my backpack. Then I grab scissors and snip the paper with Hunter's name on it into teeny-tiny pieces and throw it away. You can never be too careful!

I check my watch. Hunter will be done with baseball practice in an hour.

I set my timer.

Homework time! I sit at my desk and pull out my math homework.

The time passes quickly.

Bzzt! Bzzt! Bzzt!

I turn off my alarm and grab my backpack.

Showtime!

I hope Hunter likes his *charmed* charm!

Then a funny feeling washes over me.

Am I like the witch who gives Snow White a poisoned apple?

Answer: *Of course not! I am a GOOD witch!*

Mostly.

I run to the mirror and swab strawberry lip gloss across my lips. Then I review Melanie's flirting advice in my head.

Flash my smile,

flip my hair,

have big eyes . . .

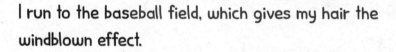

I've got this!

I run to the baseball field, which gives my hair the windblown effect.

Check!

I put my hand to my brow to shade the sun. Hunter's practice is winding down. His teammates walk off the field, but Hunter stays behind to collect baseballs. I wait on the sideline for my prince.

He's sees me!

Eeeee! I wave, and he waves BACK!

I walk toward him. "Hi, Hunter!"

I flash my smile and make BIG EYES, which requires opening my eyelids as wide as possible and then holding them like that.

It's not as easy as it sounds.

You ever try to keep your eyes wide open without blinking?

It's torture!

"Hey, what's up, Heidi?"

I strain to keep my BIG EYES in place.

Then I hold out my fist, slowly unfold my fingers, and reveal my gift. "I saw this charm at the bookstore and thought of you."

Hunter picks up the charm and admires it. "Wow, Heidi, this charm will look great on my backpack! Thanks!"

We walk off the field together. Hunter picks up his backpack and attaches the charm. "Looks good—*right*?"

I nod, still keeping my eyes open as wide as possible. (I confess, I shut them for a sec when he was attaching the charm to his backpack.)

Hunter slides his backpack onto his shoulders. Then he gives me a funny look. "You have really *BIG* eyes, Heidi!"

I step back.

Isn't that what Little Red Riding Hood said to the wolf? *My, what BIG eyes you have!*

Maybe I should tone down the big-eye thing a teeny bit.

Hunter gives me a little nudge. "See ya at dinner!"
Then he heads over to join his teammates, who are
drinking water and eating orange slices.

"See ya!" I answer.

As Hunter approaches his teammates, they all move
out of his way, like they don't want to be near him.
I overhear them talking too.

"Here comes McCann," one kid says. "Let's go!"

Then all his teammates turn their backs and walk off. They leave Hunter all alone—as in *isolated.*

Whoa! The charm is really working! But I feel a little funny about it again.

I shake the feeling off.

Come on, Heidi! Don't second-guess yourself! Remember, this spell is all about LOVE!

It's about bringing you and Hunter TOGETHER.

But this spell is also about isolation.

But it's for a good cause! I defend myself to myself.

Right?

BLINDED BY LOVE

When I get back to the room, Melanie is standing in front of the mirror *as usual.*

"Like my new outfit?" she asks. Melanie has on a pink pleated plaid skirt with a white top and a gray cardigan.

Three words: *Cute and trendy.*

"It looks really good on you, Mel!" I tell her.

Melanie twirls and her pleats fan out. "New outfits are such a mood lifter!"

Then she goes back to admiring herself in the mirror.

"But you know what's *really* weird?" she asks.

I plunk onto my desk chair. "What?"

Melanie holds out the edges of her skirt, like she's
going to curtsy. "When I picked out this outfit,
I wondered if Hunter
would like it."

Melanie lets go of her skirt, and it falls back into place. "But when I put it on tonight, my first thought was, 'Ew, Hunter McCann—what did I ever see in him?!'

"Isn't that SO bizarre? How could I have been SO into him?

"And then *blammo!* So OVER him?"

She shakes her head in disbelief.

I look down and pretend to be very interested in what's inside my backpack.

I don't want Melanie to see the smile on my face.

And wow, I can't believe she doesn't like Hunter anymore!

I know it's just the spell, but it's almost too good to be true!

And it means only one thing: **now Hunter will be MINE!** This is followed by the faint sound of evil laughter in the back of my head.

Okay, control yourself, Heidi!

Two words: *Act normal.*

"It's not *that* weird, Melanie," I say. "That's the way crushes go, I guess. One day you're into the person. The next day you aren't. My mom calls it puppy love."

Melanie puts her hands on her hips. "And what's *puppy* love?"

I draw a heart in the air with my fingers. "Puppy love is a really intense, romantic crush that usually doesn't last very long."

Melanie lights up like I've just given her the most insightful explanation ever.

"That's IT!" she cries, turning back toward the mirror. "I feel better already! I just couldn't figure out what had happened to change my mind so suddenly."

Melanie heads for the door. "Come on. Let's go to dinner." I give my hair a quick brush, and we walk to the cafeteria.

When we get there, Hunter is sitting all by himself.

There's not one other person sitting at our table—not even Jenna! Melanie and Isabelle take off for another table too.

"Hey, Heidi!" Annabelle calls from the sandwich bar. "You want to get sammies and take them *you know where*?"

Sunny is waving at me too.

Normally I'd love to go to our Secret Loft with them, but tonight I'd *rather* have a romantic dinner alone with Hunter.

It would be the first time I'd have him all to myself!

Annabelle comes over and pulls me. "Come on, Heidi! We made you a sandwich and everything!" She drags me to the hallway.

Oh well, it's not like my spell on Hunter is going to wear off right away.

And this will also give me a chance to fill Sunny and Annabelle in on **my latest strategy to get Hunter.**

They're *not* going to believe it!

When we get to the vending machine, a teacher walks by. Sunny sticks change into the slot and presses a button. A pack of chips drops to the bottom. Sunny grabs it.

It's just enough time for the teacher to get out of sight.

Phew!

Then I reach behind the vending machine and pull the lever. We slip inside and clump up the wooden stairs to our hideout.

We sit on the hay bales and unwrap our sandwiches.

Sunny still has a sort-of scowl on her face.

I know she's mad at me, but I don't know what I did.

I sort of feel like I should apologize, but I'm not quite sure what to say yet.

I guess I'll have to keep ignoring it for now.

"Wanna hear the latest news about Hunter?" I ask.

Sunny and Annabelle give each other a weird look. Then I remember that my friends may not want to hear me drone on about Hunter anymore. So I zip it and let Sunny talk first.

"We have something to tell you about Hunter too," Sunny says.

I swallow uncomfortably. That's weird.

What could they possibly have to say about Hunter?

Sunny bites her bottom lip.

"Heidi, I don't know how to say this, but for some reason, Annabelle and I don't like Hunter anymore.

"Maybe it's because you talk about him a lot, but whatever it is, we can't stand him."

Annabelle nods. "We're so sorry, Heidi. We hope this doesn't hurt your feelings, but just the mention of Hunter's name is a total bummer."

My friends stare at me to see my reaction. And I can't help it; I burst out laughing.

Sunny and Annabelle look at me with confused expressions on their faces.

Laughing is definitely not the reaction they were expecting.

"I'm sorry to laugh!" I say when I've caught my breath.

I quickly fill them in on the Love and Isolation spell I performed on Hunter.

My news doesn't go over well.

Annabelle jumps off her hay bale.

It looks like she's going to roar, like that ferocious MGM lion at the beginning of *The Wizard of Oz*.

Three words: *I'm legit scared!*

"That is SO *LOW*, Heidi!" she shouts.

And Sunny has her hands cupped over her mouth.

The size of her eyes gives "*BIG EYES*" a whole new meaning.

"WHAT?" I cry, feeling like a convicted criminal. "I only wanted to give myself a better chance with Hunter!"

Annabelle folds her arms. "That was a TERRIBLE thing to do to someone!"

Sunny nods in agreement. "What you did was heartless, Heidi. Do you even realize what you've done?

"You've made it so Hunter has *NO FRIENDS*, except for YOU, who wants Hunter *all to herself*.

"Honestly, Heidi—you don't deserve Hunter."

OUCH. That really hurts.

I cover my face with my hands. What Annabelle and Sunny have said is true. I never thought about what it would be like for Hunter to be isolated from *all* his friends.

I'd hate it if somebody did that to me!

My friends are right.

I don't deserve Hunter.

Now I feel like dirt.

No, I feel worse than dirt.

I feel like garbage with flies all over it.

I'm the poop emoji without the happy face.

If I were a tool, I'd be a toilet brush.

To top it off, I feel sick to my stomach. And here's the total truth: **somewhere in my heart I knew this spell was wrong all along,** but I ignored my better judgment the whole time. I just wanted Hunter to like me SO BADLY.

Let's face it, **selfishness has turned me into an evil witch.**

But the thing is, **I really want to be a** *good* **witch** . . . and a good friend.

I realize there's only one thing for me to do!

I HAVE to get that charm back and reverse the spell before Hunter becomes a total outcast and drops out of school.

I hope I'm not too late!

I jump off the hay bale. "You two are right. I gotta go! Talk to you later."

And hopefully my friends *will* **talk to me later.**

As I head for the stairs, I suddenly hear Sunny

in my thoughts. *I can't believe you could be so mean, Heidi!*

I stop and glance at Sunny over my shoulder. She gives me a dirty look.

So where are you rushing off to? I hear her think. *Your special magic lessons with Mrs. Kettledrum?*

Sunny's face looks sad and angry at the same time.

Then I realize something!

Sunny is JEALOUS!

But there's no time to address this right now. I have to help Hunter first!

"Gotta go!" I cry, and take off down the stairs.

Well, it's official: I now understand what it means to be blinded by love.

DARK
MAGIC

I run to Hunter's dorm and pound on his door. **He doesn't answer!**

I race to the Barn and check the cafeteria, the store, and the student center. **No sign of him anywhere!**

I run to the baseball field. I have to bend over to catch my breath after all this running. **But he's not here, either!**

My eyes fill with tears.

Where could he be?

Maybe he ran away!

Oh, please NO!

I have to keep looking.

I check the School of Magic, the gym, and the auditorium.

Still no Hunter.

Then I jog to the library. My sneakers squeak as I race to the circulation desk.

"Ms. Egli, have you seen Hunter McCann?" I ask breathlessly. She looks up from her computer. I wipe the tears from my face.

"Are you okay, Heidi?" she asks, handing me a tissue.

I wipe my eyes and blow my nose. "I'm fine, but I *must* find Hunter. It's an emergency!"

Ms. Egli pats my hand gently. "Now calm down, Heidi. He's in one of the study cubbies," she says, pointing. "But why would you want to talk to *HIM* anyway?"

I roll my eyes. The spell even works on the teachers.

This is really, really, really, REALLY bad.

"It's a *looooong* horrible story." I turn and make a beeline for the cubbies.

No stopping for hair flips this time.

"Hey, Hunter!" I whisper, trying to sound normal.

Hunter looks up from his homework and smiles. "Wow, are you actually speaking to me, Heidi? It seems like everyone in the school has suddenly shut me out."

I stand there breathing heavily, like Darth Vader after a relay race. "Of course I'm still talking to you!" I say in between breaths. "Maybe you're just having an off day."

He sighs. "I hope so, but I'm beginning to suspect that I may be under a spell of some kind. I sense dark magic, but I haven't learned how to handle it yet."

Gulp.

I had forgotten about the power behind the black feather, which Hunter selected at the Feather-Picking Ceremony. It means he has the natural ability to detect evil and keep it away.

Oh no! Is he going to bust me?!

I hope not!

Two words: *Play dumb!*

"Why would anyone want to put a spell on *you*, Hunter? You're one of the nicest kids in the whole school!" I say.

Hunter looks down at his homework. "Thanks, Heidi," he says. "So what's up?"

I take a deep breath.

You can do this, Heidi.

"Um, you know that baseball-glove charm I gave you?" I say as cheerfully as possible. "May I have it back?"

Hunter drops his pencil onto his notebook. "Why do you want it *back*?

"Are *you* mad at me too, Heidi?"

I put my hand over my heart because I'm pretty sure it just broke in half.

"Oh no, Hunter! I'm *not* mad at all!"

I feel like all the evil characters in every animated movie I've ever watched, all rolled into one.

"I just need to borrow the charm for a few minutes. I, um, want to show it to someone. I *promise* to give it *right back.*"

Wow, what a poor excuse, but it's all I can think of right now while my mind is spiraling with guilt.

Hunter reaches for his backpack. "Okay," he says sadly. He looks for the charm on his backpack.

"Oh no!" he says.

My broken heart stops beating. "Oh no— *WHAT?*"

Hunter lifts his backpack so I can see. "The charm is gone!" he says. "It must have fallen off. That's too bad. I really liked it."

I gasp and go straight into freak-out mode.

OH NO!

What if I can't find the charm?!

Hunter will be doomed FOREVER.

"It can't be GONE, Hunter! Maybe it fell onto the floor!" I drop to my knees and begin to crawl around the area where Hunter is sitting.

It's nowhere to be seen.

I hop back to my feet.

"Okay, tell me where you've been today since baseball practice," I grill him.

Hunter looks at me funny. "What do you mean, *where have I been today?* We're basically in all the same classes, Heidi! Other than classes, I've been to my room, the cafeteria, baseball practice, and here."

I grab Hunter's notebook and pencil and write down all the places he's been. He watches me in total confusion, but I *have* to find that charm!

Hunter's entire life is on the line.

"Have you used the bathroom, and if so, which ones?" I press.

Hunter raises his eyebrows. "Heidi, you're making this into a much bigger deal than it is. I'll just get another charm at the campus store. Don't worry about it!"

But I *am* worried about it.

I'm *terrified.*

My whole body is shaking.

I feel like the main character in a disastrous romantic movie that is clearly *not* going to have a happy ending.

I gotta get out of here before Hunter realizes it was ME who cast a spell on him.

He gives me a sideways glance.

Oh no, he's going to figure it out!

"Are you okay, Heidi?"

I'm definitely not okay. I drop his notebook and pencil onto the desk.

There's only one thing left for me to do.

BOLT.

FREE TO BE ME

I hurry toward the door with my eyes fixed on the floor. I look everywhere for a sign of the charm, but there's nothing—not so much as a candy wrapper.

Why did I have to make the present I gave Hunter so small?

I should have given him a book **or maybe a bright, flashing neon sign** that no one could ever lose.

I run from classroom to classroom and look under every desk, chair, and table.

Nothing.

And since no one's around, I tiptoe into the boys' bathroom. There's nothing in there, either, except for those weird urinals.

Ew.

I jog back to the baseball field, and this time I go into the boys' locker room.

No boys—*thank goodness*—and no charm.

Merg!

I head back to the Barn and check under the cafeteria tables and around all the food stations.

One word: *nada.*

I sit on a bench outside the Barn to rest and think.

The charm has to be on this campus *somewhere*!

But what if somebody found it **and *kept it*?**

I feel helpless.

Maybe I should confess what I've done to Mrs. Kettledrum.

No, only as a last resort.

Mrs. Kettledrum would be so disappointed in me. She might even take away the privilege of private magic lessons with her. I'm so deep in thought that I don't even see Sunny walk up to me.

"Hey, Heidi," she says in a glum voice. I look up.

The last thing I need is for Sunny to scold me for being such a terrible person.

She slides her hands into the pockets of her jeans.

"I was just playing Four Square, and Hunter came over and **nobody would let him play,**" she says. "**He looked so bummed.** Isabelle has been in the king square ever since dinner."

I look down at my sneakers. "Sunny, I never meant for any of this to happen. I just wanted a little time alone to get to know Hunter and for him to get to know me. I wanted us to have a relationship, but all I got was a bad situation-ship."

Sunny nods understandingly. At least she's not as mad at me as she was earlier. "I know you didn't mean to hurt Hunter or me—"

Sunny suddenly stops talking when she realizes she's revealed more than she meant to, but honestly, I needed to hear her say it.

I pat the bench. "Please sit, Sunny. I know you've been upset with me. Does it have to do with my private magic lessons?"

Sunny nods and sits down. She wipes a tear from her eye.

"I'm upset because I've been struggling with my magical classes *and* my spells."

She turns and looks at me. "Remember when we were little at Castle Spell Cove and I was teaching *you* about magic?"

I nod. "Of course I remember! You were the one who taught me how to move objects, and I'll never forget how patient you were with me.

"You also comforted me when I didn't know what my magical gift as a witch would be.

"You had all those things before I did."

"Thanks, Heidi. I know it sounds silly, but I got so jealous when I heard that Mrs. Kettledrum singled you out to work on your magic skills.

"And you knew I was feeling down about how things have been going for me, and you didn't seem to care or remember.

"All I've ever wanted is to be the best witch I can be, and now it seems like you've left me in the dust. . . ."

I hang my arm around Sunny's shoulder. "Sunny, this is not a race! You're an amazing witch, and you're here to learn how to be an even *more* amazing witch.

"And I promise to share everything I learn from Mrs. Kettledrum with you, and you can share everything you learn with me too!"

I hold out my arms and give Sunny a huge squeeze.

"We're going to be the two most amazing witches Broomsfield Academy has ever known, **and we're going to do it *together.***

"I'm sorry I haven't been there for you lately.

"I promise to be a better friend. To you and to everyone else."

And I mean it.

It's time for me to remember what's important, and that's my friends.

Obviously I've done something terrible to Hunter. And I haven't been a good friend to Sunny or Annabelle this week. I haven't been truthful with Melanie either.

Sunny smiles the sunniest smile I've seen from her in days. It makes me feel so much better.

But unfortunately, my troubles are *far* from over and it's beginning to get late.

"I'm so sorry, Sunny, but I have to go. Hunter lost the backpack charm I gave him.

"And if I don't find it, I won't be able to reverse the spell—or should I say 'curse.'"

Sunny looks at me thoughtfully. "Just remember, Heidi—you picked the gray feather, which means you bring a sense of light to darkness and a sense of balance to imbalance."

I lay my hand on my backpack, which is where I keep my gray feather. It's in a baggie, in a small separate pocket, so it doesn't get smooshed. I carry it with me everywhere, but I hadn't thought about it in relation to my current dilemma with Hunter.

"Honestly, Sunny, I feel like the *opposite* of everything that feather represents."

Sunny laughs. "Well, you may not always think things through, Heidi, but it doesn't mean you can't turn this problem around." Sunny stands up. "I have to go too, but I'm glad we talked. And I'm sure the charm will turn up—just bring some balance into your thoughts."

She winks as she walks away. Sunny is right. My thoughts have been completely out of whack.

But how do I bring a sense of balance back?

I pull my gray feather out of my backpack and shut my eyes.

When did things get so out of control? I ask myself.

I listen quietly, and the answer comes easily.

When I developed a MAD crush on Hunter.

Ever since I met him, I've thrown all reason out the door. How could I have ever thought that making Hunter *friendless* would be a *good* thing?

Answer: because I was only thinking about *myself*.

Okay, so how do I fix this mess—besides finding the charm and reversing the spell? And that's when I face the truth.

You can only fix it when you stop obsessing about Hunter. If he likes you THAT WAY, then you'll know. If he doesn't, then accept it and move on. I sigh deeply.

I don't like this answer, which is probably why I've been avoiding it for so long. I make a promise to myself then and there. If Hunter doesn't want to go out with me, then I'll let him go.

I open my eyes and feel strangely relieved. That's when I see Ava O'Connor walking by. She stops.

"Are you taking a nap, Heidi?" she asks.

I rub my eyes. "Not exactly."

Ava plops onto the bench beside me. "Well, I took your advice about spells," she says. **"And thanks to you, now my spells are working!**

"And I'm getting more confident all the time."

I smile at Ava's good news. "Glad I could help."

Ava wrinkles her forehead. "Is something wrong, Heidi?"

I wave her off. "Oh, it's nothing. I just lost something important to me—that's all."

Ava stands up. "Well, did you check the lost and found?"

I sit up. "The WHAT?"

Ava laughs. "The lost and found, silly. It's in Crawford."

I stuff my gray feather into my backpack and leap to my feet. I gasp. Of course a school would have a lost and found. Kids lose stuff all the time!

Duh! "I never even thought of it! Thanks, Ava!"

Then I jet to Crawford and run up the stone stairs to the main office. I grab the handle on the door and pull.

Aaack!

It's locked!

I jerk the handle back and forth, but the room is closed up for the night.

Nooooo!

I slowly walk back to my room.

This is going to be a *lo-o-o-n-g* night.

In the morning I skip breakfast and go straight back to the lost and found at Crawford. The lady behind the counter is the same one who gave me my name tag on the first day.

"Has anyone turned in a baseball-glove backpack charm, today or yesterday?" I ask her.

The lady leaves the counter and comes back with a big brown box. "Would you like to take a look?"

I sprint around the counter and rifle through the box. I find hats, gloves, scarves, sweatshirts, sunglasses, but no charm. Then I take each item out one by one.

Still no sign of the charm.

I'm doomed.

I dump everything back into the box. Something flies from the arm of a T-shirt and swishes across the floor. I glance to see what it is.

"EEEEE!" I squeal.

It's the charm! The lady shushes me
as if we're in the library.

"I found it!" I cry, holding up the charm.

My eyes water with happiness. "He's *SAVED!*"

The lady picks up the box. Her heels click on the floor as she walks away. If she's wondering why I care so much about a backpack charm, she gives no indication. I take off for my dorm room.

I open the door and call Melanie's name. No answer. **She's not here—*thank goodness*!** I pull out my *Potent Potions* book and read the Love and Isolation reversal spell.

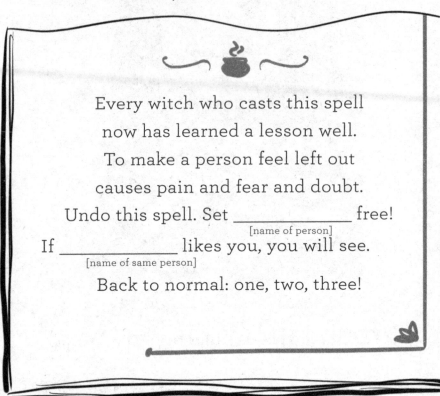

Every witch who casts this spell
now has learned a lesson well.
To make a person feel left out
causes pain and fear and doubt.
Undo this spell. Set _____ free!
[name of person]
If _____ likes you, you will see.
[name of same person]
Back to normal: one, two, three!

I wish I'd read this BEFORE I cast the spell, I think. **I really must start reading spells in full instead of diving into them without thinking.**

Live and learn! I take out my wand and chant the reversal spell.

Fingers crossed that it works.

I'm running late, so I have no time for breakfast this morning. I quickly put away my spell book and head to my classes.

I look for Hunter, but I don't see him anywhere.

When classes are over, I set out to find him—yet again. It's almost lunchtime, so I head toward the Barn.

Everyone's playing Four Square—EVEN **HUNTER!**

He's in the king square!

I clutch the charm in my hand and jog to the court to watch from the sidelines.

Everything seems normal until Isabelle cherry-bombs Hunter and knocks him out of the king square. Hunter slams the ball onto the ground, and Isabelle snags it from the air. They both laugh.

Those two are so competitive.

Hunter has to get back in line, so I walk over. I dangle the backpack charm in front of him. It's okay to return it to him, now that the charm is not charmed! "Look what I found!"

Hunter's green eyes light up. "Where'd you find it?"

I drop the charm into his waiting hand. "It was in the lost and found."

Hunter shoves the charm into his pocket. "Thanks, Heidi. You're the best!"

I flinch a little bit at this compliment. Deep down I know I'm not really the best.

But I'm going to be better, I promise myself.

I blush *big-time* and get in line to play Four Square, but then I realize I have just enough time to go to the mail room before lunch. As I walk away, I can hear Hunter laughing with everybody.

Phew! What a load off my mind! And honestly, after what I've done, I don't care if Hunter likes me or not right now. I'm just happy he has friends again, and hopefully I can be one of them.

I walk into the mail room, and the mail clerk brings me a letter. *It's from LUCY!* I walk outside to read it. The letter is on the cutest ladybug stationery! As I read it, it's like Lucy's reading it to me.

Heidi-e-e-e-e-e-e!!!
I cracked up so hard when I read your letter. You are UNREAL. Are you sure you didn't crash into Hunter McCutie on purpose?!!! J.K. were you mortified? Have you recovered? Was it a clash made in heaven??? I want details!

Okay, now I'm being serious. You asked for advice on how to get Hunter to like you. Well, there is only ONE surefire, time-tested, winner-takes-all way to get your crush to like you. Are you ready? It's so incredibly simple. JUST. DO. YOU. Seriously. There is nobody better than Heidi Helena Heckelbeck. And if Hunter doesn't crush on you back, then he doesn't know what he's missing!

That's it! Just do you! And everything will be fine.

Miss you SO much!
   Luv ya! xoxoxo,
Your bestie 4-ever,
   Lulu the Love Advisor

Lucy totally gets me—probably because she's known me for so long! My friends at Broomsfield have only known me for a few weeks, except for Melanie, and the truth is, we were always so competitive with each other at Brewster Elementary that we never got a chance to really know each other there. It's time to put all that aside and just be myself . . . and that means being a good friend to Melanie, Hunter, Sunny . . . and myself.

And even though I've made some major blunders this week, I've also done some great things, too, like my unexpectedly funny sense poem and my awesome spell for spells and potions class.

Plus, Mrs. Kettledrum thinks I'm an exceptional student.

What could be cooler than that?

And to top it off, Sunny and I got through a rough patch.

Okay, from NOW ON, no more trying to change or do anything crazy to make somebody like me.

If Hunter doesn't want to go out with me, then so be it.

Lucy's right. The only thing I can do well is ME.

And I may be a little quirky, but that's what I like *best* about me.

Oh yay! I'm free to be ME again!

And that means I don't have to wear lip gloss, aka slug slime, anymore!

Lip gloss is SO *not* me—well, except for sometimes. . . .

THE PERFECT COUPLE

The Halloween dance is tonight!

It took me forever, but I finally decided what to be.

Rapunzel.

I guess you could say my costume chose me.

Lol!

But one thing I've learned this week is not to take myself too seriously.

Now I can laugh at myself! Because the real me is bold *and* hilarious.

Melanie and I use magic to make our costumes **over the top.** Mrs. Kettledrum said just this one time magic would be allowed in creating our costumes, without getting a bad mark on our records. I'm **wearing a purple princess dress with a lace-up bodice and a poofy pink skirt.** I have pink satin gloves that go to my elbows. And the best part is my fake blond wig with a thick braid that goes to my knees. The braid has pink roses in it and a pink satin bow just before the bottom. My jewelry is a tiara, dangly heart earrings, and a matching heart necklace. I have sparkly sneakers on my feet, because, well, that's also *me.*

I stand in front of our full-length mirror. Melanie prances up to me. **"You look *good*, Heidi!"** she says. **"It's like a whole new you!"**

I laugh. "Thanks," I say. "Halloween is the one day it's okay to be someone other than yourself."

Melanie gently pushes me aside so she can look at herself. I'm not sure if she understood what I just said, but who knows—maybe one day she'll get it.

One word: *whatever.*

I look at Melanie's costume in the mirror. "You look so good, Melanie, like a glamour girl on a 1960s magazine cover!"

Melanie is wearing her hair in a high ponytail. She has on a daisy-print dress, with white go-go boots that come up to her knees. She's wearing sunglasses with heart frames! Melanie turns and looks at herself from all sides. "We both look amazing!

"And fingers crossed that Hunter will dance with me tonight. I like him again, you know. It was so weird how I just thought he was the worst for a few hours."

I nod. "So weird."

Then Melanie helps me with my makeup, and we head to the gym. To enter, we walk down a haunted hallway. I cover my eyes.

I may be a witch, but I'm terrified of ghosts, ghouls, and scary music.

It reminds me of that awful prank I played on Melanie the first week of school. I put a spell on our room, and creepy sounds played for fifteen minutes. Melanie got so scared, she ran out of the room.

And even though I *knew* it was magic, I still scared myself with the spell!

The gym has been transformed into an enchanted forest. The ceiling is a deep blue night sky with twinkly stars and a full moon. There are silhouettes of black trees everywhere. Little lights blink, like fireflies. And bats—*hopefully fake*—dip and dart around the shadowy trees.

Everything looks so real that I know it has to be magic.

Music plays, and there are cauldrons of punch and snacks on top of tree-stump tables. A few kids are already dancing.

Sunny and Annabelle run up to us. Sunny is dressed like candy corn, and Annabelle is a butterfly. We gush over one another's costumes.

I wave to Isabelle. She is dressed as an adorable forest fairy. Her dress is shimmery green. On her chest and shoulder straps are pretty purple flowers. She has a crown of flowers in her hair and gossamer wings.

One word: *stunning.*

It was as if the forest setting was made for her.

Then I spy Hunter.

He's wearing a superhero outfit, cape and all. He has a big letter *H* on his chest.

"*H* for 'Hunter'?" I say out loud. Cute, but not very imaginative.

"No, it's for 'help,' Melanie says. "I thought it was for 'Hunter' too, but he says his magic power is to help other people however he can. Pretty cute, huh?"

I nod. *Even Hunter's costume is adorable,* I think, and sigh.

Sunny, Annabelle, Melanie, Isabelle, Hunter, Tate, and I all dance in one big circle.

This is my first school dance, and I love it.

Then a slow song comes on.

Most of us head to the side of the dance floor, but some kids pair up.

Melanie pinches me and points. I look where she's pointing.

Whoa! Hunter just asked Isabelle to dance!

Isabelle smiles, and they walk back onto the dance floor. Hunter wraps his arms around her, and she rests her hands on his shoulders.

Am I jealous?

One hundred percent.

But I must admit that they make a great couple. They are both super-nice. They both love sports. They both laugh at each other's jokes.

And Isabelle calls Hunter "Mush."

I'm looking forward to getting to know them both more this year, and I'm looking forward to them getting to know me.

Melanie grabs my arm. "I wish that was *me* out there with Hunter," she says. "But you know what? Hunter and Isabelle belong together."

I nudge Melanie with my elbow. "I feel exactly the same way about *both* things."

Melanie turns and looks at me. "Does that mean Hunter was your mystery crush? I *knew* it, Heidi!"

I nod. "He was, but I didn't have the heart—*or the guts*—to tell you, because you were so into him too, and I **didn't want us to fight over a boy."**

Melanie laughs. "Well, I totally knew all along."

We both laugh and give each other a high five.

Then a guy dressed like Dracula walks up to me. "You wanna dance?" he asks me. I gulp and look for an exit.

I wasn't expecting to be asked to *slow*-dance!

It's a boy from my science class named Nick Lee.

I'm so nervous!

Then I look down and see that he's wearing sparkly sneakers too, only his are black to go with his vampire outfit.

It must be a sign!

"Sure," I say.

Nick takes me by the hand, and we walk onto the dance floor next to Hunter and Isabelle. He puts his arms around my waist, and I put my hands on his shoulders. We move around the floor randomly, like everyone else.

Nick smiles shyly at me, and his
braces shimmer in the soft light.

We talk, and it feels totally natural.

And that's when I know it will happen. Maybe not tonight or tomorrow, but someday I, Heidi Helena Heckelbeck, *will* have a boyfriend.

P.S. But don't get me wrong! Having a crush was pure bliss and giddiness, with a splash of self-manufactured horror on top.

And you know what?

It was totally 100 percent worth it.

DON'T MISS THE NEXT BOOK
IN THE SERIES!

MIDDLE SCHOOL
AND OTHER
DISASTERS

Biggest
Secret
Ever!

HERE'S A
SNEAK PEEK!

CLEARING YOUR MIND IS EASY, RIGHT?

Today is my first advanced magic lesson with Mrs. Kettledrum!

Eeee!

I've been waiting for this day for what seems like *forever*, but truthfully, it's only been two **absurdly** long weeks.

The coolest part is I am the **only one in my grade**—*so far*—that has *private* magic lessons.

One of my best friends, Sunny Akhtar, was a little bit jealous at first, but she and I had a heartfelt talk, and everything is good now.

Phew!

I totally understood how she felt. I know *I* would've been jealous if it had been the other way around.

These lessons are such a big step for me as a witch. All I've ever wanted is to be the best witch I can be, and now I'm on my way.

I'm positively buzzing with excitement as I walk across campus to Mrs. Kettledrum's classroom. Is it possible that everyone and everything looks extra beautiful today? The sky looks bluer! And could it be that the birds are singing only to *me*? Everyone I pass either waves or says hi— even some of the upperclassmen.

I am radiating confidence and happiness!

When I open the door to the classroom, Momo, Mrs. Kettledrum's corgi, leaps off her puppy bed and jumps into my arms. She licks me all over, which is kind of *ew*, but mostly adorable.

Ever since I did an original spell that made Momo *talk*, she and I have had a special relationship. Momo got to say all the things she'd always dreamed of saying.

Mrs. Kettledrum was super-impressed, and that's when she said I was ready for private magic lessons.

So here goes!

"Are you ready, Heidi?" Mrs. Kettledrum asks. She winks because she knows how excited I am.

"I'm SO ready!"

Then I follow Mrs. Kettledrum into her office. Momo trots after us too.

"Have a seat, Heidi!" Mrs. Kettledrum says, and points to one of two cozy-looking chairs in front of her desk. I plop onto the middle of a blue plaid cushion.

"Are you comfortable?"

I bounce on the cushion. "Yup, totally comfy!"

Mrs. Kettledrum drags the other chair in front of me and sits down.

"Then let's begin. Lesson number one," she starts. "To strengthen your mind-reading gift, and to truly be a *great* witch, you must learn how to quiet and control your thoughts in any situation. Quick, successful magic can only be performed when your thoughts are calm and focused."

I nod vigorously, but inside my head I'm thinking, *Being calm and focused are not exactly my strong points.*

Mrs. Kettledrum rests her hands on her lap. She

looks *very* calm and focused. I'm pretty sure she never gets ruffled. She adjusts her glasses. "The first thing I want you to do, Heidi, is to come up with a mantra to get your mind into a quiet, peaceful place."

I raise my hand. "What's a mantra?"

Mrs. Kettledrum shuts her eyes, like she's going into a trance or something, and then opens them again.

"A mantra is a word, phrase, or sound that calms the mind. My mantra is: *Peace and tranquility are mine.* Now it's *your* turn, Heidi. I want you to close your eyes and think of a mantra that will quiet *your* mind. Take as long as you need."

I close my eyes, but instead of getting quiet, my mind goes bananas.

Eek!

What should MY mantra be? I wonder,

What if I can't THINK of a mantra?

What if I think of one and it sounds STUPID?

What if I can't get this right?

In a matter of seconds, I've gone from a confident, up-and-coming witch, **to a complete nervous wreck.**

Two words: *Chill out!*

Mrs. Kettledrum interrupts my topsy-turvy thoughts.

"Now don't be surprised if your thoughts race around at first, Heidi. Simply take a deep breath . . ." Mrs. Kettledrum inhales slowly. "Think about something that will settle your mind. Your mantra should be a signal to yourself that it's time to be quiet. Simply let your mantra come to you.

Don't be embarrassed or shy. There's no such thing as a *wrong* mantra. Just clear your brain of all distracting thoughts."

I shut my eyes again. I'm glad Mrs. Kettledrum says racing thoughts are normal. She also understands being totally embarrassed. That helps too. Now I feel a tiny bit less self-conscious.

Okay, what will my mantra be? Hmmm.

How about "Be quiet, Heidi!" No, too basic. What about "Turn off the noise, Heidi!" Or maybe I should be like a hypnotist, and my mantra could be "You're getting VE-E-ERY sleepy, Heidi!" No, I'm not trying to take a nap. How about, "Shut off your brain!"

Ugh, I'm *so* BAD at this.

"This is HARD," I declare, keeping my eyes shut because I don't want to look at Mrs. Kettledrum. It'll just make me feel *more* embarrassed.

Mrs. Kettledrum pats my knee with her hand.

"It *is* hard, Heidi, but be patient with yourself.
It takes a lot of practice to get still and quiet.
Let's try something else. Instead of starting with
a mantra, I want you to focus on your breathing.
Breath work is a handy tool to quiet yourself down.
Now, take a deep breath in through your
nose, and slowly and gently breathe out
through your mouth."

I take a humungous breath in through my nose, and
slowly let it out.

"Not bad, Heidi. *Again.*"

I take in another dramatic breath and slowly let
it out my mouth. I'm pretty sure I sound like
an English bulldog snoring—or maybe
I sound more like Darth Vader
breathing.

And, instead of getting quiet, my mind wanders off

in *another* direction. *This is no fun!* I complain to myself. *I thought I was going to learn some REAL magic today,* like making a mountain of candy appear out of nowhere, or whipping up a new wardrobe, or zapping a trampoline into existence. Or maybe magically getting a mini fridge for my room?

"*Concentrate,* Heidi." Mrs. Kettledrum reminds me.

I nod obediently and try to stop the rant in my head.

Focus, I tell myself. *You are a calm, no-nonsense witch. You can be 100 percent relaxed*—even though you may not feel like it.

You are as still as the water on a lake at dawn.

You are as calm as a golden sunset.

You are as weird as the biggest GOOFBALL ever. I open my eyes.

"I feel silly!"

Mrs. Kettledrum leans back in her chair.

Is she disappointed in me? I wonder. ***Does she want to keep working with me?!*** *She doesn't show any signs of being mad. . . .*

Mrs. Kettledrum pulls off her glasses.

"What you're feeling is perfectly natural, Heidi. New ways of thinking can feel awkward at first. Believe it or not, one day you'll get to the place where every cell in your body is quiet. I didn't start out being calm in every new situation. It took years of experience and practice, but you have to start somewhere, and this is the start. Now let's go back to thinking about a mantra."

I clasp my hands on top of my head. "**What if I can't do it?!**"

Mrs. Kettledrum smiles. "Of course, you can, Heidi.

Now close your eyes and try again. Trust whatever mantra comes to you—even if it sounds silly."

This time, I don't let my mind spin like a Tilt-A-Whirl. And the next thing I know, something actually comes to me. My eyes pop open.

"I've got it, Mrs. Kettledrum! My mantra is: *My peace is here and now.*"

Mrs. Kettledrum claps her hands.

"Well done, Heidi! That's a wonderful mantra! You've successfully taken the first step toward becoming a better mind reader.

"Now for lesson number two. For this step, you'll need to turn your chair toward the window."

I stand up and spin my chair around. Mrs. Kettledrum shifts hers around too. We sit down and gaze out the window. Students are walking toward the Barn for lunch. My stomach growls.

Glurrpity-gloop! Mrs. Kettledrum acts like she didn't hear it.

"Okay, Heidi, I want you silently recite your mantra. Then focus on a student outside, and ask yourself, 'What are they thinking?' After that, listen carefully for incoming thoughts. Ready?"

I sit back in my chair. Mrs. Kettledrum nods once. "Begin!"

My peace is here and now, I think calmly. Now I have to pick a student and hone in on what they're thinking. *Oh wow! There's Nick Lee! He's the guy who asked me to dance at the Halloween party! He is SO cute!!!*

"Heidi, put your eyeballs back in your head and stop thinking about boys! We all know what happens when you put crushes and magic together. Things can get very hairy! Now clear your mind."

"I'm sorry, Mrs. Kettledrum! It's just that Nick is *sooo* cute! I won't let him distract me next time."

Mrs. Kettledrum looks at her notebook. She has no time for puppy love.

"Okay, Heidi, for homework I want you to practice quieting your mind. Really work on watching your thoughts so they don't wander." She hands me a sheet of paper with a bunch of hints.

"Thanks, Mrs. Kettledrum. These reminders will be really helpful."

Mrs. Kettledrum rests her elbows on the arms of her chair. "Sometimes it also helps to imagine yourself in a calm place, like the beach, or any spot that makes you feel peaceful."

I light up. "I LOVE the beach! I never thought to go there in my mind!"

Mrs. Kettledrum looks at her notes again and flips the page. "There's one other thing I'd like to discuss with you, Heidi. I believe you're advanced enough to learn Emergency Spells."

I sit straight up because I want to learn *every* kind of spell.

"What exactly are Emergency Spells?"

Mrs. Kettledrum taps her notebook with her pen. "They're spells for when something suddenly comes up or goes wrong—any kind of emergency that needs immediate attention. You won't always have access to your *Book of Spells* so these are spells you can do on the fly. Here at Broomsfield Academy the staff of the School of Magic must come up with spells on demand all the time.

"So for our next lesson, I also want you to think of emergency situations where you might need to perform a spell on the spot."

I clasp my hands. "Well, that's an easy assignment! My life is a never-ending string of emergency situations!"

Mrs. Kettledrum laughs and shakes her head. Then she looks at her watch. "That's enough for today, Heidi. Remember to practice quieting your thoughts. You'll get better at it the more you practice. And I'll see you at the assembly tomorrow."

I hop up from my chair and move it back to where it belongs. Then I give Momo some kisses on the top of her head. She licks my cheek.

One word: *Slobberific!*

"Thank you, Mrs. Kettledrum! I know I have a lot of work to do, but I feel like a better witch already."

Look out, world! Here I come!

ABOUT THE AUTHOR

Wanda Coven has always loved magic. When she was little, she used to make secret potions from smooshed shells and acorns. Then she would pretend to transport herself and her friends to enchanted places. Now she visits other worlds through writing. Wanda lives with her husband and son in Colorado Springs, Colorado. They have three cats: Hilda, Agnes, and Claw-dia.

ABOUT THE ILLUSTRATOR

Anna Abramskaya was born in Sevastopol, Ukraine. She graduated from Kharkiv State Academy of Design and Arts in 2006. Then she moved to the United States, where she's currently living in the beautiful city of Jacksonville, Florida. Anna has loved art since she was little and has tried different materials and techniques. The process of creation and seeing beauty in the simple things around her always brings her joy and the wish to share that feeling with everyone. Anna wants to believe that art can help bring more love into people's hearts. Find out more at AnnaAbramskaya.com.

Would you like to read another book about **Heidi Heckelbeck**?
You don't need magic to find one! Look for more

MIDDLE SCHOOL AND OTHER DISASTERS

books at your favorite store!

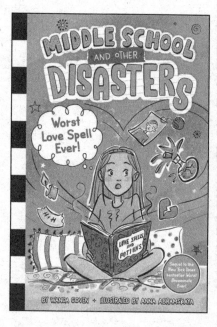